His thumb stroked the pulse on the underside of her wrist. 'Dine with me. Tonight.'

'No.' She tugged in slow motion, as if already unsure whether she wanted release or not.

'Tomorrow?' He stared into deepening violet and between them the fire flickered and stirred, and the wraith encircled them both.

'I'm working.' Almost a whisper.

He stroked her wrist again. 'Then it must be tonight.'

Huskily. Another brush of her tongue over her lips. 'What part of no don't you understand?'

But for Kiki it was too late. Too, too late. He'd touched her.

His hand held her wrist, his skin was on hers, and the two receptors were communicating, entwining like their own matrix of reality. The warmth crept up her body, wrapped around her in tendrils of mist, and in slow motion he drew her forward as subconsciously she swayed like a reed towards him.

His other hand came up and tenderly he brushed the hair out of her eyes. 'You have grown even more beautiful.'

With worship his fingers slid across her cheek and along her jaw as his mouth came down, and she could do nothing but turn her face into his palm and then upwards. To wait.

As he had with their first kiss he took her breath, inhaled her soul as she did his, and the world—the sometimes comical, sometimes cruel world—disappeared.

Dear Reader

I've always wanted to write about a dashing prince, a fairytale royal wedding and a heroine who deserves to live happily ever after.

Monaco made a big impression on me when I was lucky enough to visit last year, and I was always going to have elements of the romanticism and glamour of that fabulous tiny principality in my story. Then there is the mythology of Greece...

Which brings us to the island of Aspelicus.

Prince Stefano Mykonides has never met anyone like Dr Kiki Fender... An unexpectedly torrid love affair in far-off Australia was not kind to them when they first met...but, goodness me, do sparks fly the second time around!

So we have a cruise ship, a fabulous Mediterranean setting, medical adventure on the high seas—and then the world seems to crash for our newspaper-shy prince and his unwilling Dr Kiki.

I really do hope you enjoy visiting my fairytale countries and their romance-challenged royalty as much as I loved writing their story.

Warmest wishes

Fiona xx

Find me at www.fionamcarthur.com

THE PRINCE
WHO CHARMED HER

BY
FIONA McARTHUR

First published in Great Britain 2013
by Mills & Boon, an imprint of Harlequin (UK) Limited.
Harlequin (UK) Limited, Eton House, 18-24 Paradise Road,
Richmond, Surrey TW9 1SR

© Fiona McArthur 2013

ISBN: 978 0 263 23444 2

A mother to five sons, **Fiona McArthur** is an Australian midwife who loves to write. Medical Romance™ gives Fiona the scope to write about all the wonderful aspects of adventure, romance, medicine and midwifery that she feels so passionate about—as well as an excuse to travel! Now that her boys are older, Fiona and her husband, Ian, are off to meet new people, see new places, and have wonderful adventures. Fiona's website is at www.fionamcarthur.com

Dedicated to my prince, Ian. xxx

CHAPTER ONE

Dr Kiki Fender gazed across the blue of the Mediterranean to distant houses that clung like pastel limpets onto the cliffs of Italy and breathed in the beauty of the day.

It wasn't something she'd done when she'd first boarded the ship, but it was easier now as she listened to the delight of the newly embarked passengers.

These first few hours sailing along the Italian coast was her favourite time. But duty called so she brushed the hair out of her eyes and turned towards the hospital below. Four months of shipboard life had brought the purpose back into her life and she was so grateful for that.

Her smile slipped when she remembered it was only five days until the date she'd so looked forward to would be behind her, and then it would get even easier.

One deck down, Prince Stefano Adolphi Phillipe Augustus Mykonides tried not to think of the worst-case scenario as he rolled the unconscious wife of his brother into the recovery position. With immense relief he noted the blue of her lips improve slightly as her airway cleared.

He'd hoped Theros could stay out of trouble this week, on his wife's birthday holiday, but it seemed it wasn't so. With a sigh, the eldest son of Prince Paulo of Aspelicus, a tiny but wealthy principality in the Mediterranean Sea, knew it was his fault his brother had done something else stupid.

When he looked up at Theros his brother was as helpless as ever, his handsome face twisted in distress. 'Get the ship's hospital on the phone. Tell them it's an emergency,' Stefano said.

Theros's mouth worked silently, like a child's, and he looked shocked and incredulous as his wife began to turn blue again.

Stefano lowered his voice to a stern order. 'Now! Tell them it's a reaction to latex. To bring adrenalin.' He said the words slowly and enunciated clearly.

Theros blinked and stumbled to his feet as Stefano began to strip Marla of her skintight rubber playsuit, cursing under his breath as her breathing became even more laboured, but thankful that at least Theros had had the good sense to call him in time.

His concern lay in removing the offending clothing as fast as possible—before his sister-in-law stopped breathing. Not an easy job—which he gathered should have been half the fun. What he would have given for a scalpel...

Ten doors away Dr Kiki Fender jogged down the hallway to the largest suites, running over in her head what she knew about latex allergies. In truth Kiki was the on-call doctor for crew—not passengers—and she hoped her boss would follow quickly in case the patient was *in extremis*.

She'd hate to lose a patient on departure day, and royalty at that—very poor form. Terrible luck that Will had been on a cabin visit when the call had come in, so she was it till he came. She didn't even bother to try and imagine where this latex exposure had come from.

She'd tossed the usual personal protection gloves out from the emergency pack and donned latex-free ones, reminding herself they should use them in the whole medical centre in this current climate of escalating allergies, and had packed extra adrenalin ampoules. She carried in her hand the Epi-pen which made administration much quicker in such emergencies.

She prayed the patient's airways wouldn't have closed completely by the time her boss arrived with the rest of the equipment.

When the door opened she barely glanced at the distressed man in black shiny underwear and glanced ahead to the woman on the floor. Another man was bent over her as he struggled to extricate her legs from skintight latex leggings.

There was something oddly familiar about the shape of his head, but the woman was already unconscious and her skin was blotched with a paling red rash.

Kiki spoke to the dark hair of the man kneeling on the carpet as she bent down beside him. 'Is she breathing?'

'Just.'

Kiki glanced at the man's face and recognition slapped into her like one of the ocean white caps outside the window.

What the hell was Stefano Mykonides doing on her ship? *Lock that away, quick-smart,* she chastised herself, and quickly pinched the woman's leg to inject the adrenalin. Her eyes skimmed the almost naked woman for tiny rapid rises of her chest, aware that the movements would tell if the medication was helping. Most times with this type of shock recovery was dramatic, because the drug turned off the body's flooding allergic response like a tap.

But a tiny section of her brain was still suggesting that the Stefano she'd known was the last person who needed a threesome with a dolly bird in latex to fill his day.

She heard her boss and the nurse arrive with the emergency stretcher as Stefano leaned towards her.

'Of course I expect you to remain discreet about this event.'

She could see the pulse beating in his strong neck and a part of her responded involuntarily—and that increased her dislike. She met his eyes and tried with only some success to keep the contempt from her face. So typical. The woman was fighting for her life but it was all about how important the good name of the Mykonides family was.

She could say a few things about his good name. Instead she nodded at her patient. 'Of course, Your Highness.'

Stefano turned back to extricating Marla's foot. He was in shock—much like poor Marla without the benefit of the drug's reversal. Kiki Fender was *here* and to see her like this... As a saviour to his family, dynamic, confident of her skills as he'd known she would be. But it was not these things he remembered the most. Nor the woman who looked at him with distaste and called him Your Highness.

Before he could think what to say Marla groaned

and stirred, and his sigh of relief escaped silently as Kiki leant over and spoke near her ear.

'You're okay. Take it easy.' She looked at him and silently mouthed, *name*?

'Marla,' he said quietly, just as thankfully the last of the trouser leg came free over her foot with an elastic snapping noise. He slid the rubber suit under the seat of the lounge chair out of sight as more medical staff approached.

Kiki saw him do it and rolled her eyes at his priorities as she turned back to her patient. 'I'm going to put another needle—a cannula —in your arm and tape it there, Marla, as a precaution, but I think you're improving every second.'

The cannula slid in easily. Always a relief.

'Like I said, this is only a precaution,' she said to the dazed woman, 'in case you need further medication or intravenous fluids.' But within herself, Kiki thought the response appeared adequate from the initial dose—often the way—and it seemed the crisis was over.

She felt the trolley being manoeuvred in beside her and Stefano stood up.

He said, 'Please take my towelling robe,' and handed it to Kiki to cover the patient with.

Her nod of appreciation wasn't only for the gown for Marla, but because with him gone there seemed so much more air around the patient—and herself—more distance. Funny, that, and funny that she wasn't in the mood for laughing.

She had always had a respiratory awareness of him—like her own damned anaphylaxis—but she'd thought herself desensitised against that response after what she'd been through. Later, on her own, she would worry about that.

'Hi, Will.' Kiki glanced at the senior ship's doctor as he knelt down beside her. 'This is Marla. Severe reaction to latex. We've removed the causative agent.' She flicked an ironic glance at Stefano before she turned back to her boss.

Dr Wilhelm Hobson leaned over and took the woman's wrist to feel her pulse. 'You've given adrenalin?'

'Two minutes ago.' Kiki finished taping the intravenous cannula in place.

Marla groaned and opened her eyes more positively. 'Where am I?'

'It's okay, Marla. You're in your cabin. Just close your eyes and rest. You'll feel better soon.' She rested her hand over Marla's in sympathy. She and Wilhelm looked at the welts on her arms that seemed to be fading before their eyes. 'Good response, as you see.'

Will nodded, then wrote the pulse-rate, dose and time down on his scribe sheet while Kiki took the blood pressure cuff from the nurse and wrapped it around Marla's arm. As expected, the pressure was very low.

'In shock.' The nurse nodded as she adhered cardiac dots to the patient's skin and the sound of a racing heartbeat permeated the room. They began to assemble an intravenous line to increase the pressure in Marla's blood vessels with an extra fluid bolus.

Confident now that their patient was stable, Will stood up and faced the two men in the room. *This'll be good,* Kiki thought, and though she didn't look away from her patient her ears were tuned for their explanation.

'And who is responsible for this woman?' Wilhelm's

tone was deadly serious. But then he was serious most of the time.

Stefano had watched Marla wake up with relief and now he refocused on the room. Kiki, down on the floor with Marla, ignored him—as she should. He glanced at the man in charge—a stocky blond-headed man with a South African accent and air of command. A ship this size would need a competent senior. One who knew how to be discreet.

Then he looked to Theros. His brother stood, twisting his hands across his body, suddenly aware that he looked strange in those ridiculous shorts. His mouth worked but, as usual in times of stress, nothing came out.

Stefano sighed and stepped forward. Of course he was responsible. He had been since the moment of Theros's accident all those years ago. It did not occur to *him* to feel vulnerable, dressed only in swim-trunks, and he glanced coolly at the medic. 'I am.'

Kiki flinched when she heard Stefano's voice and realised she'd hoped otherwise. It shouldn't have mattered. Didn't matter. She'd always expected him to be more than he really was. A prince who lied and made promises he didn't keep.

She didn't wait to hear the rest. 'Okay, Ginger,' she said to the nurse. 'Let's help Marla up onto the trolley and we'll take her down to the hospital for observation.'

Fifteen minutes later Stefano paced in front of the window in his brother's suite. 'Please get rid of those ridiculous shorts,' he said. Stefano moved very slowly, with rigid control, frustrated at his brother's propensity for disaster and his own for not preventing it—and at the fruitless urge to ask why he had to deal with this. He knew why.

At seven Stefano had pulled Theros from a deep ocean pool on their island and saved his life with a boy's rough and ready resuscitation. Unfortunately Theros had been left with an injury to part of his brain from its time without oxygen. After that Stefano's young brother had not been the most sensible of boys, and later had become a handsome and lovable but childish man.

But that had not stopped Theros from diving into mischief and danger whenever he could, and as often as he was able Stefano would be the one to rescue him.

'Trouble. It will find you in the dark. Or in this case broad daylight. Is sex so tedious with your wife that you must risk her life with latex?'

Theros wrung his hands. 'No. *No*. One of her friends gave the suits to us for her birthday… We were playing. Laughing. Suddenly she could not breathe. I did not know Marla was allergic to rubber.'

'Latex.' Stefano squeezed the skin under his nose with his fingers in a pincer grip to stop himself from losing patience. He never lost patience with Theros. His father had been right to say that if only he, Stefano, had been faster at getting help perhaps his brother's brain would not have been damaged.

It was a legacy of guilt he could not shake. The job of protecting the family and Theros from ridicule had fallen to Stefano, and he had protected his brother well for many years—because he'd been willing to take up the mantle and carry it regardless of the impact on his own life.

His foray into medicine—the vocation that should

have been Theros's—had stemmed from that guilt, from his father's distress and disappointment, and from his own lack of ability to prevent such a sequela for his brother. Even at such a young age he had vowed if such a situation ever arose again he would know what to do. Unexpectedly, medicine had also provided a true vocation, and something that soothed his soul.

His father, Crown Prince Paulo III of Aspelicus, had hired a sensible woman to supervise Theros while Stefano had been away at a medical symposium in Australia earlier that year, and to everyone's surprise his simple little brother had found true love.

At his father's urgent request Stefano had rushed home from the arms of Dr Kiki Fender—but too late.

Theros had already eloped. Then Stefano himself had been involved in a serious motor vehicle accident, and during his slow recovery months had passed.

To his unexpected relief Theros's sensible wife had proved helpful in steering Theros on a more stable path, but even the most sensible could make an unfortunate mistake. So any notion of Stefano being released from his duty of care was a misconception. Theros would always need him, and he could offer no life to a vibrant and intelligent woman like Kiki, who was not accustomed to the strictures of royal duty.

In the harsh light of reality he knew that as heir to the throne he should let go of what had passed between he and Dr Fender in Australia. That was for the best.

But it seemed she had not forgiven him for his failure to return.

Theros coughed and Stefano returned to the present. His brother still waited for reassurance.

He took his fingers from his face and stared at Theros so he could be sure he was listening. Perhaps even absorbing the gravity of the situation.

'Marla could have died. Almost did.' He paused, let that settle in. 'One of you must carry an injection, similar to that which the doctor had, in case she is exposed to this product again accidentally.' He stared hard. 'You are her husband and it is your duty to keep her safe. Do you understand?'

'Yes, Stefano.' Theros chewed his lip. 'The doctor said she would be all right, though? They'll let her out of the hospital this afternoon?'

Not surprisingly, Theros had an irrational fear of hospitals—which hadn't been helped when Stefano had nearly died.

Stefano saw that fear, and his irritation with his brother seeped further away. His voice gentled. 'For the moment the danger is gone. Yes.'

Theros climbed into his swim-trunks and sadly handed Stefano his latex briefs. 'And she will be fine tomorrow, won't she? We're going to Naples to climb Vesuvius. You're coming with us.'

'My leg is a little painful.' Why must his brother love adventures that required exposure to the public? It would be so much easier on the island of Aspelicus, their island home off mainland Greece, and he had so many things that required his attention there. But his father had asked him to watch over them on this short cruise that Theros had promised his wife.

Ashore, his man could be with them. And while they were touring it would be a good time for him, Stefano, to reacquaint himself with Dr Fender.

After finding Kiki where he least expected her, he

had pressing matters to attend to. First an apology for his non-return. Past ghosts to lay.

The problem was that the woman he'd left behind in Australia had stayed like a halo around his heart. He, of all people, knew it wasn't sensible to desire a woman who did not understand or deserve the ways of royal commitment. As heir, in his country's crises *he* was the one who was called.

But still he smarted from the thinly veiled contempt in her sea-blue eyes, because he remembered the warmly passionate, fun-loving side of sweet Kiki.

The gods must be laughing at this insult to his pride. If they had been destined to meet again this was not how he would have orchestrated the moment.

Less than an hour ago—still achingly beautiful, yet transformed—she'd hated him.

She'd always been confident, sassy, and so different from the women he was usually introduced to. Of course he'd been recklessly drawn to the young doctor during his Sydney study tour to promote ground-breaking surgery at his small hospital. What a week *that* had been.

He would admit he had not behaved thoughtfully during their intense time together. Neither of them had. Everything had progressed far too quickly. They'd immersed themselves in each other for a torrid affair of incredible closeness, tucked away from the world in her tiny flat when they weren't at the hospital.

Until another crisis created by the man in front of him had required his immediate presence on Aspelicus and he had left her bed and flown out that same night.

He had spent the last few months recovering from his own accident—months of rehabilitation after he'd almost lost his leg. He'd barely been able to look at himself in the mirror, let alone consider showing himself to a woman.

But that excuse had gone now and his treatment of Kiki Fender had recently made him feel ashamed. It was another burden of guilt he found he could not move on from, because it had taken him almost five months before he was able to rule his own life again. A loss of control he never wanted to experience again.

By the time he had begun to search for her, at least to attempt an explanation, she'd been untraceable.

At first he had tried the hospital in Sydney, then her home phone, mail to her old lodgings. He did not know her friends or family. She had disappeared without a trace. Ironically to this very ship.

Tomorrow he would finish this and then fulfil his destiny for his country. Seek her forgiveness, allow himself to let go, and move on to secure the succession.

But for the moment his man-boy brother needed reassurance. Theros was playing with the legs of the latex suit he'd found under the chair and Stefano reached out and took them from him gently. 'Manos will drive you to Vesuvius.'

'Oh, good. And Marla will come.'

Theros looked childishly happy and Stefano supposed it was good that *someone* was pleased.

Later that afternoon, in the ship's medical centre ten floors below the royal suite, Dr Hobson was ready to discharge Marla.

'You can go back to your suite.' Kiki helped her sit up. 'Your observations are fine, and will stay that way if you stay away from latex.'

Poor Marla blushed again. 'No more birthday gifts that almost end it all!'

'It was just bad luck.' There was a lot of that around at the moment. Kiki grimaced with her. 'Allergies can be to anything. It could have been peanuts.'

Marla smiled. 'I'm supposed to be the sensible one. But thanks for that.'

'Hey, it was your birthday.' Kiki grinned back. 'At least now you know latex sets up a reaction in your body and you can make sure that if you ever go into hospital the staff keep you latex-free.'

The young woman nodded and stared down at the little Epi-pen in her hand.

'And be careful with that.' Kiki smiled. 'You can get into trouble if you inject it in the wrong place.'

Maria nodded.

'True,' Will said helpfully. 'I saw a man once who injected it into his thumb trying to work the plunger. It's a powerful drug and it shuts down the peripheral blood flow. His thumb fell off with gangrene.'

Kiki's eyes widened as she helped Marla up. 'Imagine what a disgruntled wife could do?'

The senior medic held out his hands in horror. 'That's true. Don't go there.'

Kiki shook her head in amusement, because Wilhelm's seriousness always cracked her up. 'Is he scaring you, Marla?'

'Only because of my husband.' The girl laughed and shook her head. 'I will not let Theros near it. I truly can be sensible.'

'Not too sensible.' Kiki smiled. 'Still have a great birthday. It's such a shame this has marred your holiday.'

Kiki couldn't help but think that Marla wasn't the

only one whose voyage had been affected. And this week of all weeks, when her emotions were already on a rollercoaster. Bummer. Bummer. *Bummer.*

Usually fair-minded, Kiki guessed she owed Stefano an apology—but it wasn't going to happen. She still didn't get why he was on his brother's holiday as his minder—on *her* ship—and was finding it hard to forget that somewhere above her head was the man she'd accepted she'd never see again.

She glanced at the ceiling above her head. Up there, larger than life and twice as disconcerting—because she might not have agreed to dress in latex for him, like Marla had for Theros, but she'd been just as weak, losing her common sense in the sensual haze they'd created together.

And as for her less than flattering thoughts of him earlier—well, he could jump off the owner's suite balcony before she'd apologise.

Ginger's offer to escort Marla to the suite was jumped on with enthusiasm. No way was Kiki going back up there. Because during the long weeks while she'd waited for his promised return, during the phone calls when she'd tried to contact him after she'd discovered she was pregnant, it had been too shameful.

There had been an unexpected lowness of her spirits when he hadn't called, and she'd been so sick and weak, barely able to function in early pregnancy, that she hadn't been able to motivate herself to do anything more about it.

By the time the first trimester had been over and she'd begun to feel more like herself again Kiki had accepted that Stefano wasn't coming back. He had clearly decided his royal status meant she wasn't good enough for him to follow up. Well, she and her baby didn't need him. All her life she'd been independent—the youngest sister to three brilliant sisters who didn't need her, with her doctor parents who were busy. The only person she'd felt connected to had been her big brother Nick. And briefly Stefano. But soon she'd have her baby and they would be a team. She couldn't wait.

But at eighteen weeks, when she'd already begun to create a nursery of tiny clothes and softest wraps, the pains had come and suddenly her baby was gone. Soon her baby's due date would pass and she would finally be able to move on. She'd promised herself.

The best thing she'd done was to come here to heal and move on to a new life.

Wilhelm wandered back into the main office. 'Marla seems very sweet.'

'She does.' Kiki blinked and came back to the present.

'Embarrassing for our royal guests, though.'

'Mortifying.' Kiki raised a smile. 'I bet her brother-in-law hated that!'

Even in the brief time they'd been together Stefano's avoidance of the whole topic of his royalty and his absolute hatred of the press had been obvious. At the time it had seemed sensible—she knew little of the life of a minor royal, which was the impression of himself he'd left her with. Not that she'd even thought about it much when they were together. As a man he'd been able to help her forget the world.

She dragged her mind back to Marla and Theros. 'It's Marla's birthday. They've been married less than a year. And Theros wanted to holiday on a cruise ship instead of their island like most of the family do.'

Will shrugged. 'So why is his brother here? Heir to the throne and all that. A bit high-powered for a minder, don't you think.'

Kiki tried for a careless shrug. 'Family name is very important to everyone, so I imagine in a royal family it would be more so.' She wasn't sure who she was trying to convince—Will or herself. 'Apparently Marla's husband has bad luck with the press.'

'Bad luck, eh?' Will raised his brows as he waved Ginger off duty on her return and shut the clinic door.

Kiki picked up her bag, but he put his hand up to stop her.

'One sec.'

She paused, looked back, and her stomach sank. She'd been afraid of this.

Will scratched his head. 'So what's going on between you two?'

'Which two?' She'd hoped nothing had been noticed. Nothing had been said. She hadn't even looked at Stefano as they'd wheeled Marla out.

Will waited patiently and Kiki felt the blush heat her cheeks. The silence stretched and she didn't like silence. That was her only excuse for being unable to extricate herself. 'You mean me and Theros's brother? Nothing.' How the heck had Wilhelm sensed that? 'I don't know what you mean.'

She switched off a computer she'd thankfully missed at shut-down. An excuse to turn away.

But the flood of memories she'd been holding back all day rose like a wave in her throat. Such rotten timing. She concentrated on her feet, firmly planted on the deck. She was *not* going under. Control re-established, she turned back to Will, who tilted his head and went on.

'Come on. I may be a bit oblivious sometimes, but the air was thick between you two and the guy was watching your neck like Dracula on a diet. Nick didn't mention you knew any royalty?'

Because she'd told no one about her stupidity—not even her closest sibling, and definitely not any of her sisters. 'Nick has nothing to do with this.' Because her brother Nick would be out for Stefano's blood if he knew what the Prince had done to his little sister. 'Stefano is a surgical consultant I worked with him briefly in Sydney during my last rotation.'

'You worked with a *prince*?'

Will looked even more interested, not less, and Kiki could feel the walls of the little clinic begin to close in on her. She didn't want to think about that time with Stefano, let alone talk about it, but her South African colleague could miss the obvious sometimes.

He proved it. 'So what happened?'

'That's all there is.' To her horror her eyes filled with tears. Not because of Stefano, but at the thought of the sadness that had been building for this past week.

'Hey. I've upset you.' Will shook his head. 'Sorry. I just want you to know I'm here to listen if you need an ear.' He raised his hands in defence. 'I promised Nick I'd look out for you.'

Don't mention this to Nick. But if she said it out loud it would be the first thing he'd do. 'I'm a big girl, Will. I don't want to talk about it. Don't need to talk about it.'

Even she could hear the over-reaction. She sighed. Too vehement.

She turned away to wipe at the tear that had slid

out against her will. 'Sorry—water under the bridge, that's all.'

'Well, if he gives you a hard time just let me know,' Will said gruffly, and she nodded and fled.

CHAPTER TWO

WHEN KIKI FINALLY fell asleep that night her dreams were filled with the sensation of being lost and alone, and always in the distance was Stefano, turned the other way and choosing not to see her.

When she woke she had tears on her cheeks, and despite the sun streaming in she was so exhausted she wanted to roll over and bury her head. Her shift didn't start until eleven but she wouldn't get back to sleep.

Through the open window she could hear the mooring crew as they secured the ship to the wharf in Naples, and she lay on her bunk and felt the ship creak and strain against its ropes.

And that made her think of yesterday's latex session gone wrong.

Unwillingly, she felt her lips curve—which wasn't a bad thing considering the night—and she knew at some stage she would have to share the story—names changed to protect the innocent—with her closest sibling. Nick would certainly enjoy the sense of the ridiculous.

She still didn't get why Stefano was on his brother's holiday.

From the brief mention Stefano had made of Aspelicus, Kiki gathered the island, once home to an ancient Greek school of physicians, a splinter school similar to the one on the more southern island of Asclepius, was a beautiful cliff-edged principality, with a harbour originally on the trade routes as a safe haven.

She'd spent hours online and discovered it had grown more Italian and French since its Greek heritage, and that its royal family were far more famous than she'd realised.

She'd been a fool. Of *course* Stefano had not returned for a brief fling he'd once had in the Antipodes.

His family had developed a stronghold in spices and teas from China, and the tiny monarchy had become incredibly wealthy. Now it was thriving on the sale of gourmet olive oil from the trees that dotted the hills, its cash flow supplemented by high-roller casinos and its own world-famous horse race along the lines of neighbouring Monaco's, which had its Grand Prix, and a borrowed idea from its neighbour to become a tax haven for residents.

On the other side of the island a sprawling low-rise hospital had gained international recognition for reconstructive surgery, with Stefano as its director.

The royal family could be traced back a thousand years, but somewhere each generation held a physician who had been available for the poorer people, as well as those who could pay.

It had all sounded incredibly romantic even from the few facts Stefano had shared with her.

She had waited for him to return.

But he hadn't.

She could remember as if it were yesterday when she'd

applied for the job on the *Sea Goddess*, her brother's old ship.

Kiki had always idolised her gorgeous, crazy showman of a big brother—the only one of her high-achieving siblings who understood her.

She never had found out what had precipitated Nick's escape from reality but for herself it was wanting something totally different from the empty nursery she'd created for a child that would never come.

She'd never shared her loss with anyone. She hadn't been able to share with the absent Stefano, and she'd thought an ordinary cruise ship the last place she would find him and reopen wounds.

Unlike her older sisters, Nick had seen she wasn't herself and cheered her on. So she'd started on the hospitality side of the ship, which had forced her to return to her usual outgoing self, the person she'd lost for a while, and she'd even started to forgive the male of the species, to laugh with Nick's friend Miko and the waiters.

Until she'd begun to miss medicine.

When the opportunity had come she'd switched roles, and the last three months had been good under Wilhelm's guidance in the ship's hospital.

It had all been fine—*until now*.

Maybe it was time to find her real calling. Hiding from the world had proved fruitless. But why couldn't this have happened next week, when she just knew she'd be stronger? She sighed.

Stefano was here and there was nothing she could do about that. It was time to move on. She'd go and see Will and ask how hard it would be for her to be replaced.

With that thought crystallising in her mind, Kiki rose from her bed and walked to the window with new purpose.

She'd put her notice in and leave as soon as they found someone to take her place.

There were still the next four nights to get through, but she'd manage that if she had a plan. She'd foolishly succumbed to ridiculous attraction last time he'd entered her orbit and that would not happen again.

Stefano woke with purpose. Today he would deal with what he should have dealt with months ago. Laying this admittedly delectable ghost was well overdue.

He'd discovered the opening times of the ship's hospital and by the time Theros and Marla had left for their day-trip the clinic was almost due to close, which suited him perfectly.

He descended the stairs almost at a jog—foolish when his hip would kill him later, and he reminded himself it was not fitting to appear too eager.

The nurse greeted him with a smile. She was the same one he'd seen yesterday, and he inclined his head at the obvious approval he read in her face. She was a handsome woman, of the type he'd used to dally with a lifetime ago, but, like a stamp on the front page of his passport, no matter where he was, Kiki had dampened any desire on his part to consort with other women.

'I wish to see Dr Fender. I am Stefano Mykonides.'

'Of course, Your Highness, I know who you are.' She smiled at him coyly, fiddled excitedly with her collar, and blushed.

Stefano smiled back blandly, curbed his impatience as the woman went on.

'But Dr Fender isn't on duty until later this morning.'

A door across the waiting room opened and the senior doctor ushered his patient out.

As the young boy and his mother walked past them the nurse said, 'Perhaps Dr Hobson?'

'No.' Stefano inclined his head at the doctor, but before he could leave Hobson crossed the room and held out his hand. They shook hands briefly.

'Ah, Your Highness. Good morning.' He turned to the nurse. 'Can you run those blood samples up to the courier, please?'

He turned back to Stefano. 'I hope all is well with your sister-in-law this morning?'

Stefano tried not to show his irritation, but he was trapped. And where was his quarry if not here? 'Yes. Thank you.' He was over discussing Theros's disasters.

Hobson glanced at his watch. 'How can we help you?'

Stefano picked up nuances and wondered why this man felt Kiki needed protection. From him. 'I had hoped to thank Dr Fender personally, for her timely assistance yesterday. I did not have the opportunity at the time, of course.'

'Of course.'

Hobson smiled non-committally and Stefano felt like gritting his teeth.

'I could convey your appreciation?'

Very pointed, Stefano thought, but he held his temper. 'Thank you, but I wish to do so myself. I will return at another time.'

Hobson didn't shift. 'I'll let her know.'

Stefano could see that the good doctor was in protection mode. He wondered just what kind of personal relationship he had with Kiki and had to admit he disliked the idea very strongly. His hand tightened on the room card in his pocket. The card bent. Disliked very strongly. He examined the doctor more closely. He was a well-muscled man, almost as tall as himself, and no doubt attractive to women.

He tested the water. 'Or I could surprise her.'

Hobson's smile appeared frozen on his face. 'I think she has had enough surprises.'

Stefano had to give the man respect. Loyalty was a good thing, and despite his own misgivings he could not grudge Kiki her friend's championship. Though his cousin, who owed Stefano many favours, *did* own this shipping line.

His fingers loosened. *Relax. Let it go.* He, too, cared that Kiki was not upset. 'It is not my intention to distress her.'

Hobson met his gaze head-on. 'Good.'

Enough. His day had soured and the pain in his hip from his reckless descent down the stairs was annoying him. 'And good day to you, Dr Hobson.'

Stefano pressed the button for the lift with remarkable restraint, not stupid enough to brave an ascent of twelve floors despite his sudden frustrated desire for explosive energy. The lift doors opened and, as if conjured, Kiki stood waiting to alight.

'Just the person.' Wonderful how good humour could be instantly restored. 'One moment, please, Dr Fender.' He could not believe his good luck—finally—and gestured for her to wait. With a relief he was careful not to show he stepped in beside her as she hesitated.

Kiki couldn't believe her bad luck. So close to being safe. 'What if I was on my way to work?'

He shrugged those shoulders that still made her weak at the knees. Damn him. It was so hard to not to stare and just remember.

'I have been told you are not working for a few hours.'

His voice always had made her mouth dry, and now was no exception. What was the scientific reason for that? She searched a little desperately for distraction as she watched him press the lift button for the sixteenth floor.

Of course he had looked for her in the hospital. If only she hadn't run down for a quick chat with Will.

The doors began to close and for a moment she did consider diving out before the doors shut, like some female secret agent with a barrel roll in her repertoire—but she'd just look awkward, and probably get sandwiched by the doors.

Or, a hundred times worse, he'd put out his hand and touch her, and she wanted to avoid that at all costs. That was what had happened the first time. He'd laid his hand on her arm to help her from the car and she'd woken up in bed with him. And stayed there for a week.

That left the smart mouth as her only defence. 'So where are we going?' As if she didn't know.

He didn't reply, and she remembered that. The frustrating habits of a man used to answering questions he felt inclined to and ignoring the rest. A prince with his own agenda unless it was for his family. Lucky him.

She stared straight ahead at the doors of the lift as if they'd magically open and she could float out to safety somewhere in the stairwell. She could feel his eyes on her.

'Why are you on this ship anyway, Your Highness?'

She heard him sigh. 'Do you call me that to annoy me?'

Now she glanced at him. Sugared her voice. 'Is it working?'

He looked at her from under his own raised brows, and then in the ultimate retaliation he smiled. Blinded, she felt it rip open the wound she'd healed so diligently over the last months aboard ship. *Blast, blast and double blast.* She needed to get away.

She'd fallen in lust with him the first time she'd seen him. Only lust. Love wouldn't have ended as it had.

Stefano had smiled at her then, as if they shared a secret, when she'd been late for her last surgical day in the operating theatres because of car trouble. He'd been a guest consultant of her boss, and should have chastised her like all the other consultants would have done, but instead he'd shown her surgical techniques she'd never thought to witness.

Later, he'd bought her coffee, plied her with cake to replace her missed breakfast, and invited her to ride home with him at the end of the day. When his hand had touched hers she'd been stunned like a landed fish, all big glassy eyes and floppy with desire.

And she knew where that had led.

The flicker of the number lights speeding upwards brought her back to the present and her sense of impending danger grew exponentially. This wasn't sensible. Or safe. Though she wasn't sure who she was more afraid of. Him or herself.

'I don't want to go anywhere with you.'

She thought for a moment she'd actually hurt him. There was just a flicker behind his eyes… But that was a joke. Instead he sighed as if she were a troublesome child, or probably just a troublesome subject.

'I will not keep you long.'

'Well, I know *that*.'

This time he did flinch. She saw it. Good, he felt guilty—even though he didn't know how guilty he *should* feel. But she was tired of scoring points or second-guessing his intentions. She just wanted to forget she'd seen him again and re-grow the scar tissue so she could complete her healing.

When the lift stopped she planted her feet more solidly on the spot. He waited for her to pass him and when she didn't lifted his hand to direct her. She stepped out of his way and back against the wall so fast his hand fell.

'No.' She licked dry lips. 'Goodbye, Prince Stefano. Have a good life.'

There. She'd said it. What she hadn't had a chance to say nine months ago. Now it was done. Finished.

Except he didn't get out, and the silence lengthened.

Without direction from them the lift doors shut and the chamber began its descent to another level.

His voice was mild. Slightly amused. 'So, are we to ride up and down in the lift all day until you wish to get out?'

She stepped further to the left of him. 'Leave me alone, Stefano.'

He didn't lift his hand again, but his voice reached out to her. She tried to imagine a soft ball of cotton wool jamming her ears to mute the sound—it didn't work.

'Is a few minutes of your time so much to ask? A chance to apologise, explain a little, and then we may part as friends—or less, if that is what you wish.'

She didn't know how much more of this power struggle she could take before those damn tears she could feel prickling behind her eyes made their escape.

She could get out on another floor, stride away, and then spend the day dreading what could be over in a few minutes if she just faced it. Over and done with. Great theory, but what if it wasn't? She still wasn't sure who she trusted least.

The silence lengthened. The lift stopped and began to go down further. 'For goodness' sake. Must you get your own way in everything?' She stepped forward and stabbed the light for the sixteenth floor. The little button rattled with the force. 'Get it over with.' The lift whooshed upwards again.

Stefano winced. This was not how he had expected it would turn out. A polite thank-you, a question as to whether she was well, an apology because he had had to leave so abruptly the last time they'd been together, and—most importantly—he would see that he was not as attracted to the flesh and blood woman as his imagination had assured him. Then he could move on to his duty.

In fact, to his discomfort, the desire for Kiki back in his arms, and most assuredly in his bed, was growing stronger by the second.

Perhaps he should have stepped out of the lift on his own after all. But how was that going to help his predicament?

The lift doors opened again and he extended his arm against the doors to hold them. 'After you.'

'Are you? Not again, I hope,' she muttered, and he had to bite back the smile.

This was the woman who had captured his attention over that long-ago week. With her tiny rebellions that always startled him out of his self-assurance, the rapier wit that amused him with its irreverence, the unpredictability of Kiki with the crazy name and so alluring body.

He was in trouble. But, then again, so was she.

CHAPTER THREE

KIKI PRECEDED HIM into the suite and glanced around. Very grand. Split level. She hadn't noticed much yesterday—too many other things had been going on. Like a woman critical with shock. Like Stefano reappearing beside her. Like a hundred memories she didn't want to remember.

She kept her back to him. 'Must be cosy, sharing with a married couple.'

'Their suite is very similar. Next door.' Kiki could hear the smile in his voice. The lock clicked. 'This is mine.'

Why did she feel there was emphasis on 'mine'? She squared her shoulders and faced him. Why did he have to look so damned amazing. 'So let's have our little conversation and then I'd like to leave.'

He ignored that. The ignoring thing again. He prowled over to the drinks cabinet. Turned to face her and asked mildly, as if they did this every day, 'Would you like something to drink?'

No, but she wouldn't mind something in her hand she could fiddle with—or throw in defence.

Kiki circled the plush sofa and sat on an upright armchair. 'Thank you. Soda water.'

He smiled. 'You were always so confident.'

She ground her teeth. 'Until I met you and thought the sun shone out of your tailbone.'

Of course he ignored that too. 'You always had fire when roused.' They both heard the echo of a similar word. Was that *a*roused?

He held out her drink and she took it carefully, so as not to touch his hand. Again his gaze met hers and she looked away. Knew his gaze never left her face. She could tell even with her fierce concentration on her glass.

His voice drifted over her like a wraith, encircling her, pulling tighter. 'But still there is more. Yesterday you were incredibly efficient. Practised. Calm. Capable. All things I knew you would be.'

She didn't want to hear this. She wanted out. 'Why don't you cut to the chase, Stefano? Why are you here on this ship?' And, more to the point, 'Why am I here in your suite?'

He stepped closer. 'The truth?'

She shrugged, trying hard to disguise the fact she was getting more spooked by the minute. 'Novel idea, I know.'

He came to stand in front of her chair. 'I could not forget you.'

'Spare me.' *Please don't say that,* she pleaded mentally. 'It took you nine months to figure that out?' She winced. Unobtrusively she eased back in the seat to create a little more space. Now she could inhale his aftershave, just a wisp, and it was true: the sense of smell was the one true memory.

He looked down. Apparently sincere. 'I did search for you.'

'Then you're not very good at it, are you?' She'd still been in the same flat for the next five months. Waiting. Hoping he'd at least call back. Until she'd woke up to reality. 'Tell me. When did this fictitious search occur?'

Thankfully he stepped across to the window that looked out from the stern of the ship and she could breathe again.

The glorious picture window framed the blue of the ocean, the trail of the wash from their ship, and the haze of land off to the east. And the outline of Stefano's magnificent frame.

'It was many months before I could begin. Only now, through chance,' he added more thoughtfully, 'or fate, have I found your whereabouts...'

He'd waited *months*! Not in a hurry to find her, then. Four weeks after he'd left she'd discovered she was pregnant. Another fourteen weeks and she'd been desperate for him to call so she could share her confusion, share her joy at the promise of finally feeling as if she belonged to someone, share her fears and hopes with the father of her child. Instead she had been completely alone.

But not as alone as she'd been when her baby had slipped away one silent night. The doctor had said her baby had a cardiac malfunction, a missing part so the growth could not progress, and she had accepted that—with grief, like the lacking in the relationship it had come from. The grief had been worse because in the beginning she had been ambivalent about its coming. Had thought more of the complications than of her own child until it had been too late for fierce regrets.

And the due date was next week.

The ever-present ache squeezed in her heart. It was

time to go before her control let her down. 'Great. Thanks for that.' She stood, glanced at him up and down. 'You look well. Don't seem to be pining. I think you'll survive.'

He stepped back into her comfort zone. 'Is Hobson your lover?'

They were standing chest to chest, a pulsing fission of air between then, and she almost missed the question.

What? Where did this guy get off? But stoking up her anger was a good idea. Much better than sadness. Anger made her feel less trapped. Less baited by his need for control at this moment. Less weak.

Flippantly, with an airy wave of her hand, she said, 'He's one of them.'

The flare in his eyes stunned her.

'Then his position has become vacant.'

She blinked. 'Don't be ridiculous.' She sat down again in shock. Any other man and she'd think he was joking. 'You can't do that.' Wrong thing to say. She knew it as soon as it was out of her mouth.

He didn't even have to say it out loud. Of *course* he could do it. The power of the Mykonides in the Mediterranean had never been in doubt.

Her turn to back-pedal. She'd suspected he had this side, had just never been shown it before. 'Of course Will's not my lover.'

Stefano cursed his temper, something he usually had an iron control over, and wheeled away to look over the sea again. The sea was unpredictable today, like his feelings for Kiki, and just as dangerous. More bad behaviour on his part. But despite that he felt his shoulders relax a little. He had not believed Hobson was her lover, but the concept had been gnawing at him since his visit to the ship's hospital this morning.

So what else had she said that was not true. 'Is there a man in your life at the moment?' He could feel the beast within him stir at the thought, and it didn't escape his notice that he had no right to ask such a thing.

She opened her eyes wide. 'Is there a man in yours?'

Little witch. 'Why are you baiting me?'

She glared back at him. 'Because apologies and good wishes haven't appeared on the menu and that was what I was promised.'

She had a point. And again he was behaving badly. Why did this happen with the woman he wanted to liaise honourably with?

He paced and came to stop in front of her. 'I sincerely apologise for leaving without explaining my reasons.'

She nodded. 'And the phone calls you didn't return?'

Those he could not remember? 'I did not get them.'

'Perhaps not.' Her tone said she didn't care any more and she put her glass down. 'I accept your apology. Thank you for my drink.' It was untouched.

So that was that. The degree of disappointment seemed out of proportion to what he'd expected. The wall between them was too great for them to part amicably but his expectations had been optimistic. At least he knew where he stood. It was time to move on. To duty.

She stood again. 'Goodbye, Stefano.'

But as she passed him his hand reached out of its own volition and captured her wrist. Her skin was soft and supple and so fragile. She froze and lifted her eyes to him. Limpid pools. He'd forgotten how her emotions changed their colour from brilliant blue to dark violet when she was aroused. Or angry. Which was it?

His thumb stroked the pulse on the underside of her wrist. 'Dine with me. Tonight.'

'No.' She tugged in slow motion, as if already unsure if she wanted release or not.

'Tomorrow?' He stared into deepening violet and between them the fire flickered and stirred and the wraith encircled them both.

'I'm working.' Almost a whisper.

He stroked her wrist again. 'Then it must be tonight.'

Huskily, With another brush of her tongue over her lips, she said 'What part of no don't you understand?'

But for Kiki it was too late. Too, too late. He'd touched her.

His hand held her wrist, his skin was on hers, and the two receptors were communicating, entwining in their own matrix of reality. The warmth crept up her body, wrapped around her in tendrils of mist, and in slow motion he drew her forward. Subconsciously she swayed like a reed towards him.

His other hand came up and tenderly brushed the hair out of her eyes. 'You have grown even more beautiful.'

With worship his fingers slid across her cheek and along her jaw as his mouth came down, and she could do nothing but turn her face into his palm and then upwards. To wait.

As he had with their first kiss he took her breath, inhaled her soul as she did his, and the sometimes comical, sometimes cruel world disappeared.

Her hands crept up around his neck and his hands slid down, until he cupped her buttocks and pulled her in hard against him. With the taste of his lips on hers, she could feel all of him, rock-solid against her, familiar, and then his mouth recaptured hers in the way only Stefano's could.

She moaned against his lips, her mind blank in the thick sensuality only he could create. She forgot all her intentions, all her reservations, and when he lifted her shirt, swept it over her head, sighed at her lace-covered breasts, she gazed up in a sensual mist of buried memories at the man she'd dreamt about last night.

He carried her across the room and she hooked her legs around his hips. Her mouth was on his, starving for the fuel of life she'd missed, as they went up the stairs to the loft bedroom in a haze of heat and hunger and primitive surrender.

The fog parted briefly as he lay her down, stripped off his own shirt. She could see the muscled perfection of his chest, the fine sprinkling of dark hairs and the nipples erect with his desire. Quickly he protected them both. And before her brain could function sensibly he was beside her, stroking, murmuring his delight, kissing her mouth as if he would never stop, and she was lost again despite the insistent whisper that warned she would taste remorse later.

She felt a long ridge of unfamiliar scarring on his thigh, a myriad of smaller ones, and her hand stilled. But he swept her up again before she could investigate further and the moment was lost in the maelstrom.

Stefano felt the swell in his chest, the furnace of desire for this slip of a woman who, until he touched her, could hold her own. Then she was his. He sensed it. Tasted the victory he hadn't known he burned for until it was upon him.

Clothes had fallen away, skin melted into skin, and heat seared between them as they reacquainted, shifted, joined. Together they cried out, until the sound died in the little death and she lay beneath him, limp and spent in his arms.

Then he moved again, slowly, savouring every tiny moment, every gentle trail across pearl-coloured skin, every cupping of mounds and exploration of hollows. And always he returned to her mouth, her honeyed mouth that he could never have enough of, until the beat grew faster, the hunger more desperate, the climax more shattering, and again they collapsed.

Replete for now, in awe, still confused by the speed and urgency that had carried them both, he lay back with his arm under her, hugged her close, smiling and sated.

For the moment.

Until the drop of a tear landed on his bicep.

'You are crying?' Stefano felt the dagger of shame and turned to see her face. Kiss her hand. 'I have hurt you. God, no. I am a beast.'

Kiki was in shock. She'd done it again. One touch and she'd lost all will. How could that be? She was no young and foolish teenager, swept off her feet by a handsome man. She knew what he could do. Had wept buckets at his hands before. If she didn't get out now she would lose what shreds of self-respect she could gather from the clothes strewn around the floor.

'I have lint in my eye. It's okay.' She eased out from under his hand and inched to the edge of the bed.

He sat up, the sheet falling from his chest, his hand out. 'Let me help you.'

'*No.*' It was sharp and panicked, and she tried again in a calmer voice. 'No. Thank you. One moment.'

A plan. She had no plan except to escape. Not to let him touch her again. Her feet touched the floor and she scooped up her underwear on her way down to the bathroom, padding down the stairs in bare feet to where her shirt lay at the bottom of the steps like an abandoned child. She scooped it up. Hopped on one leg as she slipped on her panties.

God. What had she done? How had it happened? At least he had used protection—but then they had done that last time. She would get a morning-after pill. Make sure.

All stupid thoughts when really she should be worried about escape and remaining undetected by a ship full of people who knew her. She opened and closed the bathroom door noisily, yet didn't go in. Instead she hurriedly pulled on her bra and her shirt and slipped out through the door as soon as she was dressed.

Outside she pulled on her sandals and smoothed her clothes. To top everything off if somebody saw her leave the suite of a passenger her job would go. And she was due at work in an hour.

On the crew level she passed Miko, her friend from her first early days on the ship, when she'd been more than a little lost. He was another of her brother's confidants, and the restaurant manager on the *Sea Goddess*.

She ran her fingers through her hair. *Nooooo*, she must look a sight. Miko raised his eyebrows, smiled sardonically, and walked on without saying a word. Did she look like a woman who had just left a man's bed? Kiki hurried to her cabin in the crew's quarters and as she went she groaned.

* * *

Stefano groaned too.

She'd gone. He knew it. And now, instead of finding resolution, they were in deeper trouble than before. What the hell had happened? He pushed the heel of his hand back into his forehead. *Idiot!*

It had been like this the first time he saw her. She'd arrived breathless, like a beautiful, vibrantly exotic bird, grabbing his attention so that he'd barely been able to concentrate on surgical technique. Her fierce intelligence had shone joyfully out of the most beautiful eyes in the operating theatre, like the Mediterranean Sea at sunrise, and he'd been lost.

His time with Kiki in Australia had blurred into a golden haze of laughter and loving and lust, and even his responsibility to Aspelicus had faded for a brief while.

When duty had called he'd fully intended going back to reassess it all properly—discover where it led. He had thought it would be a matter of days before his return, but first there had been the accident, then the months of rehabilitation, when the chance of losing the use of his leg had hung in the balance. It had all kept him away. As if the gods had intended they should both suffer for too perfect a match.

By then she'd disappeared. And more crises had arrived. Slowly his mind had been torn from her as well—except for that tiny halo in his heart.

But it was bad that he had hurt her. Profoundly. He could see that now, and deeply he regretted it. The trouble was that it seemed if he had an opportunity to hold her again he had no choice but to take it. Hold her. Lose himself. This had to stop. This was not healthy.

Not wholesome. Because the way he felt at this moment he would destroy them both before he could stop the way he wanted her.

The next morning, as the ship moored at Civitavecchia for Rome, the clinic was quiet.

'You okay?' Will looked at Kiki with concern.

She forced a smile. 'I must have eaten something that disagreed with me.'

Like a morning-after pill that sat on her stomach like a rock. She couldn't rid her mind of the distant warning that this had been the only chance she'd had to carry Stefano's child again. She hated that thought.

'Take the day off sick. I've got nothing planned. We'll manage.'

'No. I'll be better with something in my stomach, perhaps. It's fine. I'll stay.'

'Why?' Will gently propelled her out into the empty waiting room and towards the door. 'Go. Lie down. Read a book. You're allowed five sick days a year and you haven't had one.'

She didn't want to go back to her cabin to beat herself up. To go over in her mind relentlessly how she'd allowed herself to be seduced, had reciprocated in the seduction. It was an even tougher pill to swallow.

But she did feel miserable—and not just mentally.

'Okay. But I'll swap a day. I'll do one for you next week.' She looked at Will's concerned face and felt bad, but relieved. 'Thanks. I'll see you tomorrow.'

'Do you want me to get them to send up some food?'

'You're a sweetie.' She offered a wan smile. 'No. I'll wander. See if anything looks appealing.'

At least she needn't worry about running into Stefano in the public dining rooms. Far too plebeian for a prince. Though, to give him his due, he just avoided public places himself—he had no grudge against them.

Stefano had never played on his royal privileges or his power with her.

Except yesterday, when he'd thought she was sleeping with Will.

That had shocked her. There had been real possessiveness in that threat, and she didn't understand why.

If he'd wanted her, truly wanted her, then surely he would have moved heaven and earth to get back to her. How hard was it to pick up a phone? E-mail? Even a stamped addressed envelope would have been nice.

That was the crux of everything. She hadn't meant enough for him to follow through and say he wasn't coming back. Though, looking at what had happened between them yesterday, maybe he'd just expected to drop in every couple of months or so and be back in her bed.

She groaned and climbed the stairs to her room. As expected, when she got there it closed in around her.

Nope. She couldn't stay here.

Swiftly she shed her white uniform and stood in front of her small wardrobe. Brightly printed sundresses made her want to shade her eyes, and she winced her way along the rack until she came to black. Perfect. It suited her mood. Suited her intentions if the absolute worst happened and she came across him.

CHAPTER FOUR

STEFANO HAD LEARNED from last time. When he telephoned the hospital, as expected, the nurse answered.

'No, Dr Fender is not working today. In fact she has just left to get something to eat.'

She thought perhaps in the main dining area.

Stefano had not been through the main entertainment and restaurant areas. Apart from an early-morning swim in the lap pool just before Marla's unfortunate medical crisis, he'd avoided the other passengers. A discreet perusal of the common areas would not hurt him.

Kiki looked at the array of food, grimaced, and chose a banana. She knew they were good for hangovers and, while she hadn't had any alcohol, the Stefano hangover left her all kinds of miserable. Her belly rolled and she glanced at her watch. Not time yet for her next anti-emetic. That was the problem with morning-after pills. The nausea that accompanied them was pervasive.

As she wandered back out to the pool area a redheaded pre-teenage boy scooted past, almost knocked her down, slowed, and called sorry over his shoulder. He spied his brother, obviously a twin because they looked so similar, closing in, and put on speed again.

To have that much energy... 'Hey, slow down,' Kiki called after him.

Just then his brother slid into sight, didn't make the corner, lost purchase as he rounded a post at speed, and before Kiki could tell him to slow down it was too late!

The second boy's feet flew from under him and, unable to save himself, he slammed his head of red hair into the steel pole.

Kiki stood, stunned, then her mind clicked into gear. She took two quick strides and fell to her knees to bend over him, but the boy had clearly been unconscious before he hit the ground.

Kiki hailed a passing waiter who'd missed the action and sent him off speedily to summon further medical aid. Apart from him there were very few people near her.

Until the last passenger she wanted to see appeared and strode over.

For the boy's sake she was glad. For herself less so. She ignored the surge of nausea as Stefano approached, and forestalled any comment other than on the present. 'Did you see him hit?'

Stefano nodded. 'If he has not fractured his skull he is very lucky. I will take the neck as we roll.'

Stefano placed his hands either side in case of spinal injury, and together they turned him carefully onto his side to keep his airway clear.

Just then his brother reappeared around Stefano's shoulder, his freckled face screwed up with fright. 'Is he okay?'

Kiki recognised him with relief. 'What's your name?'

'Mikey.'

'And your brother's name, Mikey? And the number of the cabin your family's in?'

The terrified boy stuttered out that his name was Chris, and the number, and Kiki repeated it to make sure she had it right.

'Okay. Go get your parents. I'm a doctor. Your brother hit his head and knocked himself out. We'll take him down to the ship's hospital as soon as the stretcher gets here and we'll meet you down there with them.' The frightened boy nodded and sped off. 'Slowly!' Kiki cautioned him, and she saw him reduce his pace to a jog.

Stefano's mind rolled back the years to a moment he'd never forget. A time when he too had been terrified at his brother's lack of response. The feeling of being powerless to prevent an accident, to prevent disaster. His father's constant reminder that *he* had been the responsible one weighed heavily even now. It was no wonder he needed to feel in control as a man. But he could feel that control slip away now, as this boy sank deeper into unconsciousness.

Kiki must have seen the sadness in his eyes, because she paled and he recognised the moment when she too felt the presence of impending disaster.

'You think he's critical?' she asked quietly.

'Theros was like that as a boy. Always rushing.'

She frowned, missing the context—for which he was glad. No doubt she was impatient with his latex-loving sibling right now.

She shook her head and concentrated on the boy. 'I heard the impact. Horrible. Wilhelm should be here with a stretcher ASAP, but he'll need to be shipped out.'

'I agree.' Stefano lifted the boy's eyelids one at a

time to see his pupils and frowned. 'If we are that lucky.'

Will and Ginger arrived and Stefano helped them ease on a spinal collar and slide the boy onto the stretcher on a spine board. Within minutes they were all crammed in the lift on their way to the hospital, and Stefano could feel his own heart-rate increase as he watched tiny ominous changes in the boy. A flicker of a tremor in one finger. The shudder of an indrawn laboured breath. Nobody spoke as the doors shut and they all watched their patient.

He saw Hobson look at Kiki. 'He'll need to be shipped out immediately.'

Stefano checked the pupils again. 'There may not be time. Already one pupil is dilating.'

Will shuddered. 'So fast?'

'It happens.' He glanced up at him. 'Do you have the equipment for burr holes here?'

'Craniotomy? I guess so.' Will looked at Ginger, who nodded. 'But I've never done it. Cranial surgery's not a common thing on cruise liners. We should chopper him out from the wharf. Faster than an ambulance.'

Stefano shook his head. 'The preferred option is retrieval, but I do not like the look of this. It should be considered just in case.' They all knew even that took time.

'Kiki says you're a surgeon. If it's burr holes will you stay? Supervise?' Will asked.

Stefano nodded. He could not leave and never know.

'Of course.' Then he saw the limbs on one side of the boy begin to tremble, faintly at first, and then with greater intensity as he began to convulse. Stefano helped Hobson hold him desperately to keep his cervical spine stable until the seizure ended.

Chris's breathing slowed, stuttered, and the boy's condition deteriorated further even in the short time it took to descend to the hospital. Stefano's heart sank. To them all Chris's prognosis had begun to look horrifyingly bleak.

Kiki fought back the horrible feeling they would be too late and helped Ginger steer the trolley from the lift as soon as the fit ceased. That was when she realised the boy's parents had arrived before them.

Stefano hadn't seen them. 'The fits will get worse as the pressure builds.'

'What will get worse?'

A bluff redheaded man hurried across to them with his worried wife and Mikey in tow. Kiki gently guided them aside as the others pushed through to the hospital.

'Hello, I'm Dr Fender.' She took the man's hand. 'Is Chris your son?'

Worried grey eyes met hers. 'Yes. Mikey said he hit his head.'

Kiki nodded. 'It was a very nasty fall. I saw it. Dr Hobson and Dr Mykonides are going to examine him now. While they're doing that we need to know if Chris has any other illnesses, or allergies that we should know of. Has he ever had any operations?'

The father looked at his wife and she shook her head, fear huge in her eyes as she realised the gravity of Chris's accident. 'Is he going to be all right?'

Kiki could only pray. 'I'm sorry, I can't answer that. He's very ill. He may have fractured his skull and torn a vessel inside his head. It looks as though he is building a collection of blood that is pressing on his brain.

Our first preference is to fly him out by helicopter from the wharf because his condition is so critical.'

She looked at them, deeply sympathetic, but sensible to the fact they needed to know what was going on.

'As soon as the doctors have examined Chris we'll know if we have time to transfer him. Dr Mykonides is a passenger, but also a very experienced surgeon. He will know what is best.' Chris's mother began to weep silently and Kiki drew them into the waiting room. 'I'll send the nurse out to see if she can get you something while I find out what going on.'

'Thank you, Doctor.' The boy's father drew his wife and son under the shelter of his arms and Kiki felt the tears sting her eyes.

'I'll be as quick as I can.'

The father's voice followed her. 'Take all the time you need. We'll wait.'

She nodded, left and prayed as she hurried into join the others. Surely Chris would recover. She knew how she'd felt the pain of grief when she'd lost her tiny baby, but couldn't imagine the worry *they* must be feeling.

Wilhelm had booked the retrieval team but they would be thirty minutes before arrival at the earliest.

'We'll lose him if we wait.' Stefano examined the depressed skull fracture on the rapid X-ray they'd taken while Kiki read out the boy's blood pressure and pulse. He shook his head. 'I give fifteen before brain damage is irreversible,' Stefano confided in Kiki quietly.

Kiki agreed. 'Systolic blood pressure's rising, widening of pulse pressure, and his pulse is slowing.'

The pressure inside the head was compressing

Chris's brain down towards the base of his skull. At some point it would do irreversible damage.

Will nodded. 'Let's do it.'

Kiki looked at Wilhelm. 'I'll talk to the parents, get consent, while you and Stefano get scrubbed. The nurse can get him set up in the suture room. We can make this happen fast.'

Chris's parents stood up quickly when Kiki hurried into the waiting room.

'A helicopter's on its way but Chris has pressure from the blood building very quickly on his brain. Already his blood pressure is high and his pulse has slowed right down. Dr Hobson and the surgeon, Dr Mykonides, agree it is imperative to operate now to re-lieve that pressure. I'm sorry to have to tell you there is a real risk Chris might not survive his arrival at the hospital if we don't do something now.'

Chris's mother put her hand over her mouth and hugged her husband, and Kiki saw the lump shift in his father's throat as he gathered his wife in. 'Then do it.'

Kiki passed them the consent form, and the father signed quickly. 'They're setting him up now. The object is to make small round holes in Chris's skull to let the pressure out and repair the bleeding artery before the brain is damaged. It's an emergency lifesaving proce-dure. We may be too late. Do you understand?'

'Just save him. And afterwards?'

'A medical team will arrive to stabilise him and transfer him to a hospital neurological ward.' She squeezed the mother's shoulder. 'Do you have any other questions?'

The father looked at his wife and other son. 'Not now. He's in your hands. Hurry.'

Kiki nodded and did just that.

By the time she was back in the tiny operating theatre Chris's skull had been shaved on the side of the fracture and draped to create a sterile field. Will and Stefano were preparing the area with an antiseptic solution.

'Consent signed. They'll ask questions later. Please go ahead.'

The ventilator machine was breathing for him, but no anaesthetic had been used because the boy was deeply unconscious. It would be Kiki's task to monitor that and Stefano handed Will a syringe of local anaesthetic for the skin incision just in case.

Will hesitated and Stefano waved him on. 'Let's go. Inject the site. Make a three-centimetre incision through the skin. Separate the fascia.'

Will did so and the boy didn't move. His breathing sounded mechanically in the room and Kiki was glad they'd had time to intubate, because at least they could keep him going until the pressure on his breathing centre was released.

She'd never seen the operation before, and Stefano kept a commentary going as Will performed the surgery.

'Control the bleeding with the diathermy. Use the retractors now.' They could all see Will's hands shaking but Stefano's voice was rock-solid. 'Exactly. Yes. Now drill the hole with the hand drill two centimetres above and behind the orbital process of the frontal bone.'

Will's hands shook more, and Stefano leaned across and steadied him.

'This is good. You will be an old hand soon.' He glanced at Kiki. 'How's our boy going?'

'Holding his own, just. Pulse now forty. BP one fifty on forty.'

'We have a minute or two at the most. Faster drilling.'

Stefano's eyes looked even grimmer and Kiki wondered if he was frustrated by Will's nerves. She couldn't tell, and wondered if he might throw legality to the wind and take over.

Will continued with the procedure.

'Watch for the release of pressure.' Just as the words left Stefano's mouth a thin, powerful stream of blood shot upwards high off the table from the collection in Chris's head.

Will jumped back as it slowed to an oozing trickle and Stefano murmured, 'Good. Pressure is released.'

Will shuddered. 'No wonder his observations were going off.'

'Speed is essential. Now we find the bleeder.' Stefano pointed with tiny mosquito forceps. 'There it is. Tie it off.'

Will leaned in. Tying off vessels was something he was good at.

'Good. Now bandage for transfer.'

Half an hour later the emergency team loaded an almost stable Chris into the helicopter.

Stefano walked across to where the other boy watched the transfer of his brother. His red hair stood on end from his agonised raking and fat tears rolled down his freckled face. He knew the turmoil ahead and Stefano's heart ached for him.

Mikey looked up. 'It's my fault. I shouldn't have teased him. He wouldn't have been so angry.'

Stefano put his hand on the boy's shoulder, squeezed the bony ridge as Mikey dashed his hand across his eyes. 'It is hard to watch. Especially for you as a twin.'

Stefano sighed as he fought back his own images. He couldn't bear the thought that this boy would go through the remorse he had.

'My brother was sick like yours once. And I tell you it is *not* your fault your brother hit his head. Boys run and chase, and things happen we have no control over. It could have been you that fell and he would not have been able to stop it happening.'

Mikey looked away from Chris to the man beside him and he did not look so woebegone. 'You think?'

He knew. 'You did everything right by getting your parents to the hospital. We might not have saved your brother without them being there so quickly.'

Mikey sniffed and rubbed his nose with the back of his hand. 'I ran. I did what the doctor asked me to do.'

Stefano nodded and patted the boy's shoulder again before he lifted his hand. 'You did well. Your brother is strong and he has you.'

They watched the helicopter pilot start the rotors and soon it was in the air. Chris parents came across to shake Wilhelm's hand and thank Kiki and Stefano, and then with Mikey they climbed into a waiting taxi that would take them to the hospital.

Will turned to Stefano and nodded. 'Thank you.' He sighed ruefully. 'Though I wish you could have done it.'

Stefano smiled grimly. 'No. It is better to have the experience. One day another boy may need your skills, and doing it yourself can never be replaced by watching. There were only seconds between the same result for you or I.'

Will nodded again and glanced at the ship that shadowed them on the wharf. 'I need to report to the Captain.' He glanced at Kiki, and then Stefano, but held his tongue. 'See you later.'

Kiki felt as if she'd been run over by steamroller now the tension had been relieved by Chris's transfer, and suddenly it didn't matter that Stefano was the only one left beside her.

She saw him in a different light. She'd watched him go out and talk to Mikey and hadn't been able to help overhearing some of his words.

Today Stefano had been kind, thoughtful, and a steady teacher. As much as she hated to admit it, he'd seemed like the man she'd fallen for. He'd been great with Will. And he obviously cared about the trauma to both boys.

So what had happened to them? Her and Stefano? Nine months ago? Didn't she deserve the same consideration that he now gave to an unknown family?

It didn't make sense that he'd stepped out of character and left her with no further contact after the week they'd had without a good reason.

Was there more she didn't know?

'Perhaps we should talk?'

Stefano smiled ruefully and she felt the mirror of her own response. 'Somewhere public?'

'Lord, yes.' No way was she going anywhere near his bedroom.

CHAPTER FIVE

STEFANO STEERED KIKI to the rooftop coffee shop and chose a corner table behind an exuberant fake palm. Kiki didn't mind because she was feeling particularly pale and not very interesting as nausea elbowed its way back into her consciousness now she had time to think about herself.

Stefano frowned as he noticed her pallor. 'Do you wish for something to eat?'

Kiki's stomach rolled and she winced. 'No, thank you. Just black tea.'

'You are unwell?'

He leaned towards her and again she recognised the tang of his cologne. This time, unfortunately, it wasn't her stomach that reacted. Something much more visceral stood up and waved.

She leaned back. 'Something I ate.'

'Strangely, my appetite for food is also absent.' His eyes darkened and she hated that—because she could feel herself weaken...and waken.

There was that damned glint in his eyes that she couldn't help but smile at. 'Stop it.'

He shrugged those shoulders and she looked away. He said, 'So, I admit it is good to see you, Kiki.'

She wasn't falling into that one. 'No comment.'

His brows went up teasingly. 'So comment on something else.'

Umm. Something safe. 'Do you think Chris will be okay?'

He shrugged, not with unconcern—she could see that—but with a glimmer of hope despite the contrariness of life. 'I will keep in contact by phone, but I think the surgery should have done the job before damage, and his vitals maintained perfusion. Tomorrow will give a good indication.'

She'd known that. But still it was good to hear the hope in his voice. A silence fell. She could feel his eyes on her.

'I think there is more you wish to discuss with me.'

Well, he was right there. She should get it out and finished with. Dispel the questions that were beginning to eat at her all over again. She drew a deep breath and looked back at him. 'Why didn't you contact me after you left so hurriedly?'

The waitress arrived, took their order, smiled and batted her eyelashes at Stefano. He allowed her to walk away, and when she was out of earshot he leaned forward and said the last thing she'd expected.

'I was in an accident. Unconscious and then physically disabled.'

He had her full attention as she searched his face. Now she could see them. Tiny lines that hadn't been there before, a few strands of silver through his black hair at the side of his face. She had a sudden memory of that ridge of scar on his hip she'd fleetingly discovered yesterday. Her fingers fidgeted with the salt shaker, tensed, ached to reach across and touch his hand in sympathy. But luckily she wasn't that stupid.

She let go of the shaker and retreated her hand to the edge of the cloth. 'What kind of accident?'

'Motor vehicle. I spent several months in hospital. By the time I was discharged and could begin to sort what needed to be sorted you were gone.'

He laid his hand palm up on the table, as if to signal he knew she wanted to comfort him with touch. Like a coward she shifted her hand into her lap, and his fingers closed over themselves emptily as he sat back.

When she didn't say anything he said, 'By the time I could look, I could not find you. I thought perhaps you wished it that way.'

He watched her face and she saw the moment he understood that she had, actually. By then.

So would she tell him about her own little visit to hospital? No. She couldn't go there now. It was all too painfully close.

'I was on ship. Had my own family stuff happening. My brother got married. I made friends here.'

He sat back further, as if to illustrate the distance between them now. 'Life went on?'

She nodded, as if everything was sweetness and light. Not the way she was feeling. 'As it does.'

'But now we meet again.'

His voice dropped like that cloak around her shoulders and she mentally shook herself at the spell he could weave just by words and cadence and his very presence.

Harden up, she reminded herself, and sat straighter in the chair. 'Life is still going to go on, Stefano. You'll get off the ship. I'll sail away.'

He leaned forward. 'It does not have to be that way.'

'Yes, it does.'

She wasn't stupid. She'd learnt her lesson. Yes, he'd been sick for a couple of months, but that had been months ago. No contact after that because she didn't count enough. Well, she deserved better than that.

'Because we're from two very different worlds.'

It would always be that way, which was why she wasn't going to put her heart out there to be stamped on again. Or be seduced into his bed for the next few convenient days.

Now his voice was more formal and his expression more difficult to read. 'So are you always going to be a ship's doctor?'

But she didn't need to read him. She just needed to get out of here. 'No. I'm ready to move on.' Now. Literally. She glanced at him. 'Funny how I feel so unsettled today,' she said dryly.

'And where would you move on to?'

She shrugged. This whole scenario was surreal. They were like two acquaintances, chatting over a cup of tea. 'Maybe I'll go for experience. There's always the other extreme to this—foreign aid medicine. My brother's wife worked in a tent city in the Sudan. Or I could move into family medicine with Nick and his wife back in Australia.'

He nodded. 'It is very beautiful there.'

'They're having twins.' She shut her mouth with a snap as hurt from the past rose in her chest.

Her eyes prickled. She did not want to talk about expected newborns with Stefano.

She looked away hurriedly, in case he saw something in her face, then went on brightly as she drained her tea. 'Or I could go back to Sydney to another hospital. The family home's still there.'

'I see you have put some thought into this.' He looked pensive.

She didn't like to tell him it was only since yesterday. His fault. All she had to do was resign.

The nausea rose unexpectedly and she stood up. 'I'm sorry. I have to go.'

He rose also, his forehead creased with concern. 'Let me see you to your cabin safely.'

She could almost smile at that. 'I'm in the crew section. Out of bounds for passengers. So you see...' she leant on the table and pushed herself away from him '...I will be safe.'

Stefano watched her hurry away. Was she really nauseated? She looked pale—or was she upset? Did she hate him that much? All questions he would like an answer to, he mulled as he walked back to his suite. There was more going on than she had explained, he was certain of it, because deep in his gut he knew she was hurting—and he had caused it.

It seemed it was his lot in life to hurt the people he loved. But how to ensure she would at least talk to him?

Perhaps it was time to take the Captain up on his offer to inspect the bridge.

Will sent Ginger to check on her around four. 'Will wants to know if you're up for dinner in the officers' mess tonight. Captain's request.'

Kiki sighed. 'Bloody Stefano.' She didn't think she'd said it out loud but apparently she had.

Ginger looked suitably shocked. 'Kiki! I haven't been here long but I've never heard you swear.'

Stefano hadn't been here then. 'Sorry, Ginger. But stick around for the next three days and you might hear more.' *Oooohhh,* she'd kill him.

Ginger sighed dreamily. 'He must really like you.'

Yeah, right. 'He liked me before. For a week.' Indiscreet. She shouldn't have said that. But she guessed most people could tell they knew each other a little. Even Wilhelm had noticed. 'Stefano's bored and he thinks he can amuse himself before he disappears back to his little island.'

Ginger laughed. 'You can't really call Aspelicus a little island. It's got mountains, and flat lands—and casinos, even. And it has this massive village on the side of the volcano, a gorgeous palace, and a fab hospital.' She rolled her eyes in ecstasy. 'It's the most amazing place.'

Kiki had to laugh. 'You've obviously been there?'

'Last year. I was knocking around with the in crowd with my on-again off-again boyfriend—gossip columnist, long story—and we ended up there for the Prince's Cup.'

'A horse race?'

Ginger nodded nostalgically. 'Magical horse race they do there every year along this spit of sand at the edge of the island. Raises squillions for the hospital. And there's balls and cocktails and champagne lunches. I swear I put on ten pounds over five days.'

Ginger grinned.

'Anyway, Stefano looked pretty amazing as the host. So I guess I have a soft spot and can't get over the fact you don't want to play with him.'

Kiki rolled her shoulders and rubbed the wooden

block full of tension that was her neck. 'Because after the fun and games I'm left picking up the pieces.'

'He really hurt you.' Ginger must have heard the truth because her expression changed to one of sympathy. 'I'm sorry. Want me to tell Wilhelm you're not up to dinner?'

Kiki knew she'd have to go. 'It was a request from the Captain. I can't decline just because I want to avoid his guest.'

Ginger was still new. 'Why not?'

You just didn't do it. 'Because Stefano will blow it all out of proportion, I'll find myself in sick bay, and Will doesn't deserve the hassle.' She sighed. 'What time?'

'Seven.' Ginger twisted her hands. 'The nurses have been invited as well. Umm…do you think you could introduce me to that dishy Miko if you get a chance?'

Her friend Miko, who smiled as if he knew more than Kiki was saying. 'He's a heartbreaker.'

Ginger shrugged. 'I need someone to take my thoughts away from my ex. I'm not here for marriage. And I heard he was fun.'

Kiki grinned. 'He's fun, all right.'

When Stefano saw Kiki enter with Hobson the rest of the room faded. He thought she looked less pale than earlier, which was what he'd wanted to see. Or that was what he told himself.

'Ah, the medical staff are here.' The Captain smiled. 'But of course you have shared high drama with them already. Dr Hobson tells me your advice was invaluable.'

Through his contacts Stefano had been updated

hourly on Chris's condition and the boy was improving steadily. 'Dr Hobson and Dr Fender were instrumental in saving that boy's life. And the nurses, of course. You have a brilliant medical team on your ship, Captain.'

The Captain visibly preened. 'I'm glad to hear it.'

'Of course Dr Fender and I are old friends.' His companion straightened with interest and Stefano chose his words carefully. 'We met during a consultancy I held in Sydney last year. I fear she is concerned someone might think she's consorting unprofessionally with a passenger if she's seen too much with me.'

The Captain was eager to dispel such a thought. 'Not at all. Fraternisation does not apply with previous acquaintances.'

'I thought not,' Stefano said smoothly, 'but of course I'm glad to hear you say so.'

'No problem.' The Captain stepped forward to meet Wilhelm and Kiki as a waiter circled with a tray of champagne.

Kiki knew the Captain and Stefano were looking her way and were talking about her. Her ears were practically on fire.

'Soda for me,' Kiki said, and took the glass with a thank-you nod at the waiter as Stefano and the Captain approached. She should have asked for something with a kick. She plastered a smile on her face.

'Prince Stefano has been singing your praises, Kiki. All of the medical team, in fact.'

Kiki could play that game. Nice and impersonal. 'We were lucky to have such a surgeon to consult with, sir.'

'Prince Stefano tells me the boy is improving consistently. There is real hope he will make a full recovery. And no threat of the parents suing my ship.'

She didn't care if Stefano saw how much that news improved her evening. It was worth coming just for the information. 'That is wonderful news about Chris, sir. And of course your ship.'

The impulse to share her joy with Stefano meant she couldn't avoid looking at him any longer. Of course he was watching her when she did sneak a glance.

She searched manfully for a topic to deflect the pink that was rising in her cheeks. 'Your brother and his wife are not here, Your Highness?'

She saw his brows lower at her mode of address. 'Theros and Marla are watching the show tonight.'

The Captain nodded eagerly. 'The show is excellent. Of course the crew's pageant will be on in two nights. You must not miss it, Prince Stefano. Kiki and Miko dance.' The Captain sighed nostalgically, glanced around and gestured the restaurant manager over. 'They tango brilliantly.'

Kiki distracted herself by watching Miko cross the room. All the women smiled as he joked and nodded, more of celebrity than the actual Prince. Kiki couldn't help her smile. He was such a hoot.

'Sir.' Miko saluted and the Captain introduced Stefano.

'I think you have not met our royal guest—Prince Stefano of Aspelicus.'

Miko made a very creditable bow and Stefano nodded his head.

Oblivious, the Captain went on. 'I was just saying how much I enjoy watching the crew pageant and especially your dances.'

Miko gallantly turned to Kiki. 'It is all because of my beautiful partner. She is a feather.' He lifted Kiki's fingers to kiss her hand with consummate grace. 'You look ravishing as always, Dr Fender.'

Kiki grinned and pulled her hand away. Something made her glance at Stefano, who had narrowed his eyes at the interloper. All trace of good humour had disappeared from his face and she remembered the way he'd reacted to her quip about Will.

Kiki decided discretion was the better part of valour. 'I have someone who wants to meet you, Miko. Excuse me, Captain, Prince Stefano.' And she drew the playful restaurateur away before more damage could be done.

'Ho-ho, if looks could kill,' Miko whispered teasingly in her ear.

Kiki relaxed against him. 'You are a menace.'

Miko's voice dropped even lower. 'And you have been sleeping with the Prince.'

'Stop it.'

He shrugged. 'You have known him before, perhaps? He is very jealous.'

Jealous, or a dog in the manger? 'That's his problem.'

'And mine if he thinks you care for me.' But Miko laughed. He wasn't stupid. 'And also a problem for you too.' He shrugged as they moved out of sight. 'So why do you fight this great attraction?'

Survival. 'Because we are from different worlds and he has hurt me before.'

'And Nick knows of this?'

Kiki felt like stamping her feet. 'Why does everyone think my brother has to know about my life?'

Miko shrugged. 'Because he will kill us if anything happens to you. So it is purely selfish on my part.'

She had to laugh. 'You are so shallow.'

'That is true. But it's also true that is what you love about me. Come. Introduce me to this woman who wishes to meet me and I will let you go back to your brooding Prince.'

Kiki poked him. 'I'm sticking with you and I'm going to spoil your chances of seduction.' Kiki stopped when she found the nurse. 'Ginger, I'd like you to meet my friend Miko. I'm sure you've seen him around.'

Miko bowed. 'It is a great pleasure to meet you, Ginger. I believe this is your first cruise with us?' Miko lowered his head over Ginger's fingers and while his vision was obstructed Ginger winked her thanks.

The Second Officer approached and as Miko straightened he glanced at Kiki and grinned. 'Kiki? You are leaving us? I fear the Captain has placed you at his table.'

Next to Stefano.

The men stood as she approached and Stefano frowned away the waiter who'd moved to hold her chair.

As she slid into her seat she murmured, 'Seated by a prince. I am lucky,' and sat demurely with her hands in her lap. Stefano settled in next to her.

'Behave or I will not sit next to you.'

'You arranged it.'

'True. Because I can.' He changed the subject. 'I realise we have not danced.'

What had brought that on? Dog in the manger? 'Apparently you have to go out in public to do that.'

He sat back in his chair and regarded her. 'Not always, but *touché*. Of course I am happy to meet your conditions.' He gestured with his hand. 'After this, perhaps?'

Not likely. 'I'm afraid not.'

Silkily he said in her ear. 'And why are you afraid?'

Thankfully the entree arrived at the same time and she didn't have to answer. She turned to the person on her right.

Stefano was not altogether displeased. So she was afraid of her own response in his arms? A healthy re-spect for the severity of their fierce attraction was wise. Not fear of him, but of herself, for he had never sought to inspire anything but lust in Kiki's beautiful breast.

Stefano hid his smile and turned to the lady on his left.

The Captain's wife was Sicilian and had visited Aspelicus before. She was very pleased to be seated next to the Crown Prince. Stefano knew it would amuse Kiki to see him cornered, so he paid such flattering attention to the good lady he doubted he would be al-lowed to eat in his suite again.

Thankfully the Captain's wife enjoyed her food, and when the main course arrived he could turn to his other companion.

'The Captain tells me you are off duty tomorrow when we dock. I will be flying out to Aspelicus for the day on a matter of state that will not take long. Perhaps this could be a chance for you to see my homeland.'

Before she could decline he went on.

'We would have time to visit my facial reconstruc-tion clinic before we leave. It has facets of treatment that may interest you.'

She shouldn't be tempted, but his genuine passion for his work was clearly evident and it called to the vo-cation in herself. 'How far is Aspelicus that you can fly to do business and come back?'

He clicked his fingers. 'A mere hour's fight.'

The Captain's wife leaned across. 'You should go, dear. It's fabulous. And the Prince will look after you.'

Kiki muttered under her breath. 'That's what I'm afraid of.'

CHAPTER SIX

THE NEXT MORNING, as the ship docked in Livorno, after a night of mental flogging because she'd weakened, Kiki had to school the shock from her face when Stefano arrived at the gangway to disembark.

Dressed in a designer suit as black as his hair, with his royal chain of office flashing gold and precious stones in the sunlight, he looked nothing like the man she could lose herself in.

Her first taste of royal bling and she had to admit he wore it well. Too well.

The passengers leaning over the ship's verandas seemed impressed too, if the flashing of cameras was anything to go by.

His man opened the door of the official car and gathered her in. It was a discreet luxury sedan, so hopefully people wouldn't gawk and point at them as they drove along. She slid across the seat, suddenly glad she'd worn her best trousers and a camisole with a jacket, because even though she was off the ship it looked as if this was a day when she'd need everything she had to keep her head above the water line.

'I'm sorry to have kept you waiting.' Stefano slid in next to her, and despite the gap between them on the seat she could feel the shimmering energy field as he settled.

'You made quite an entrance.'

He narrowed his eyes at her as if perplexed. 'How so?'

And didn't she wish she hadn't started *that* conversation? 'You look very princely.'

'At the risk of being simplistic, it is my job.'

Well, she'd asked for that. But he looked so overpoweringly regal she was feeling threatened by her own insignificance. Not something she'd ever felt before. And what would it be like when they arrived at the palace, where he held considerable power?

Just the thought of feeling inferior made her spine stiffen. 'You said you have matters of state to deal with? What will I do while you attend to those?'

His gaze softened as if he sensed how unsure she was about their arrival. 'I had thought Elise, my housekeeper, could show you over the palace if you would like. She will no doubt burn your ears with her historical fervour. Elise is very proud of the island's heritage.'

So she was to be diverted to the housekeeper. That should keep her out of the way. 'She sounds interesting.'

He didn't turn to face her. 'She is, but if you are not in the mood for a history lesson you could relax in the library and browse. We have an extensive collection of original books collected by my mother.'

'Both options sound appealing.' But the history more so. She could sit in libraries any day.

Now he turned to her. Searched her face. 'I should not be long. It is a matter of signing papers that should have been ready a week ago, and the settlement of a matter which has caused my father some concern for too long. Hence my decision to be done with it today.'

The car drove onto the tarmac of the airport and eased smoothly to a stop.

Stefano glanced out of the window. 'I hope helicopters do not worry you?'

'Not that I've noticed in the past.' *Never been in one.* She was quite pleased with her nonchalant tone, but seriously, how many people chose helicopters as their basic transport?

She'd been psyching herself for a sleek little Learjet at worst, but there was not much she could do about their mode of travel now.

'I'll be fine.' Though it looked more like a large bumble bee than an aircraft.

To top it off Stefano had climbed into the pilot's seat and the lump in her throat tightened. His man opened the rear door. 'I'll sit in the back, shall I?' she murmured to herself, and allowed him to bow her into the helicopter with its royal insignia, her reluctance disguised because she'd always prided herself on her sense of adventure.

This definitely rated as an adventure. She'd bet there were hundreds of girls who would have changed places with her, and she wondered again why Stefano had manoeuvred her into accompanying him on this excursion.

As soon as the pre-flight check was complete Stefano turned and assured himself that she was strapped in before he started the engine.

As the roar grew louder the little cabin began to shake and she resurrected the deep breathing exercises she'd learnt long ago during her obstetric term. Calmness at take-off seemed a great idea.

In through the nose all the way down to the base of her lungs, hold for three, and ease out through the mouth before breathing in again. She didn't care that the breaths seemed loud in her ears and that Stefano's man must be looking at her strangely.

Thankfully after six inhalations the flutter in her chest began to ease, and when she opened her eyes that were three feet above the ground and going up fast.

Everything happened very quickly after that as they rose and turned and soared away from the helipad towards the Mediterranean Sea. The shimmer of the waves below made her squint and reach for her sunglasses in her bag, and away to her left the hull of their ship overshadowed the docks.

Islands dotted the horizon in tiny volcanic outcrops, some with soaring peaks and others quite low to the water. After nearly an hour, during which she'd begun to enjoy the bird's eye view over the waves. she realised they were approaching a larger island, shaped almost like a whale, with the hump of a volcano in the middle and three separate areas of inhabitation. A long beach on one side edged a magnificent horse racing track, and she guessed that was where all Ginger's action had happened.

They approached the soaring volcanic cliffs and flew towards a turreted castle perched in a position impossible to assail without permission. As she looked down at a ribbon of winding road that circled the cliffs she guessed that was the way to the gate. And when she saw the even tinier toy cars that clung to it she wondered if that was where Stefano had had his accident.

To the left were rolling hills with what looked like miles of olive trees and scattered small villages, and on the other side of the island it seemed there was a small city she barely saw before the sight was cut off as they approached the castle.

Her stomach rose and fell as they landed on a brightly painted H on the castle forecourt with a tiny bump, and then Stefano had lifted his headphones and turned back to her with the flash of a white smile. A man who enjoyed his time at the controls. Why would that surprise her?

The door beside her opened and she fumbled to re-lease her seat belt as fresh mountain air rushed into the little helicopter. Her companion was already out, and Stefano had waved away the person in front of him and waited with hand outstretched to help her from the cabin.

'Welcome to Aspelicus, Dr Fender,' he said formally, but the twinkle in his eye showed he was pleased to be able to share this moment with her.

She had no choice but to lay her hand in his, and of course when his hand closed around hers she couldn't help the smile she returned. She really needed to learn to avoid physical contact with this man.

'Thank you, Your Highness.' She gathered her own control and looked around. 'Your castle is very beauti-ful.' The words replayed in her head. Even the conver-sation was surreal.

'I think so.' He turned to a tall grey-haired woman who had crossed to his side. Her eyes were warm and kind and she obviously adored Stefano. 'Elise, this is Dr Fender. Please care for her this morning, until I can return.'

'Certainly, Your Highness.' She inclined her head, obviously happy to do whatever he wished.

Stefano nodded and strode off towards another stairway, surrounded by suited figures, before Kiki realised he was going away.

So much for goodbye, Kiki thought. A bit abrupt in the leave-taking department, to her mind, but maybe she was being childish to expect anything else.

Elise waved her hand gracefully towards the main sweeping castle steps. 'This way, Dr Fender.'

Feeling a little like an unwanted package, Kiki lifted her chin. 'Please, call me Kiki.' She smiled at the older woman. 'And may I call you Elise?'

'Certainly. Welcome to Aspelicus.'

They turned and began to climb the wide stone steps. Sections of the stone had been worn away by feet over the centuries.

Kiki glanced around. Everywhere the castle was meticulously maintained, from its flowerbeds to lichen-free stone. 'The castle looks old but very beautiful.'

'Some form of the castle has perched here for over a thousand years, and thankfully all generations have continued to treat it with respect and care so that it remains as strong today as it has ever been.'

Elise glanced around and Kiki had no doubt that any fault found would be swiftly acted upon.

'And has Prince Stefano's family always been the ruling family?' She couldn't believe she was talking about the man whose bed she'd left only yesterday. At that thought the heat rushed to her cheeks, and she stopped to examine a particularly ugly gargoyle and breathe back control.

Elise's voice drifted over her shoulder as she, too, paused. 'Indeed. Which is rare. They have been for-

tunate in that their sons have been most virile and capable of siring many lines.'

With a pang of loss, Kiki knew she could believe
that.

'Now, with Prince Theros happily married, there is
even more surety of the line continuing. And I'm sure
Prince Stefano will marry before the year is out.'

Kiki frowned at that little pearl of information. 'Do
you mean he *has* to marry?'

Elise inclined her head. 'It is by royal decree that
the heir to the throne must marry by the time he turns
forty.'

So Stefano must be thirty-nine. Ten years older than
her. She hadn't realised there was such a gap, but then
when had they sat and discussed mundane matters like
his needing to be married by the time he was forty
and only having a year to do it? Instead they'd made
love. Often.

Her mind darted like the birds swooping outside
the windows and she had to remind herself to be in
the moment. It wasn't every day she had a private tour
of a palace. So she tried to concentrate as they walked
through into a vaulted main entry with impressive til-
ing in glorious Italian marble that seemed to shimmer
with light. Their footsteps echoed away to the gold-
trimmed ceiling that soared to a huge dome adorned
with age-darkened seascapes in turbulent oils.

During the next hour Elise opened doors to lush
apartments filled with gilt furniture and more framed
artwork. Some of the paintings were so huge they covered entire walls, while the floors glowed with the sub-
tlety of magnificently woven rugs from the Orient.

The throne room proved the most regal, with red

silk walls, two huge portraits of a man and a woman, and an extremely ostentatious fireplace that seemed to be made out of solid gold adorned with the royal crest.

'This is where the current Prince, Paulo III, was married. That is the late Princess Tatiana.' Elise sighed. 'She was a wonderful woman.'

Kiki looked at Stefano's mother and saw her regal son in the same hooded yet beautiful grey eyes. 'And very lovely. Everything is magnificent.'

Elise nodded and led her back to the main hall. 'It is a mission I take on gladly to keep it this way. But these formal areas are not the most comfortable to sit in. These are state apartments, for formal gatherings and the hosting of foreign dignitaries.' She gestured to a side stairway. 'If you would like to follow me we will go through to the family apartments, where it is easier to relax. Perhaps a cup of tea would refresh you?'

'Thank you. Lovely.' An overused word, but Kiki couldn't help feeling a little overwhelmed.

The idea that Stefano had been so comfortable in her little two-room flat seemed ludicrous and hard to imagine. No wonder he sat blasé amongst the furnishings on board the ship. It was nothing compared to his home. And yet when they'd been alone together she'd known there was nowhere else he'd wanted to be than with her.

'The upkeep must be horrendous?'

Elise frowned. 'It is a duty and a privilege.'

Oops. Of course it was. That's what royal families and their subjects did.

They went through a set of large stained glass doors and suddenly the light and warmth of a much less formal area lay before them.

'Oh, this is gorgeous.' Kiki could see a conservatory to the side, overflowing with lush green plants, and to the left a sunken lounge with a handful of plush cushioned lounges and chairs. There were flowers everywhere, and even the artwork was modernistic and lighter, but no less magnificent.

'The late Princess, Prince Stefano's mother, refurnished this.'

'She had lovely taste.'

Elise sighed with pleasure. 'Our tiny country is fortunate that its ruling family is wise in the ways of fashion and finance.'

Kiki glanced around. *They'd have to be.* 'Very wise.'

'Yes. The family fortune has built since not long after the Doges of Venice began amassing their own fortunes. Before the family became the Aspelican monarchy one distant uncle was even friends with the famous Venetian Marco Polo, and the island became an outpost on the routes of trade and gathered the riches of silk and spices.'

Elise waved at a wall full of glorious pottery from all over the world.

'But since early Greek times always the family has held physicians. The Crown was bestowed on the first Prince of Aspelicus because he saved the eldest son of the Italian King during a fever that all had thought would carry him off.'

Elise really did love her history, Kiki thought with a smile, and encouraged the woman to go on.

'In every generation one of the family becomes a physician, and I understand Prince Stefano will be showing you his hospital this afternoon.'

'He did mention that.'

'Prince Stefano does great work.'

There was an extra thread of emotion in her voice that had Kiki turning back to look at the woman.

'Personally for you?'

'My son. After many miscarriages I bore a live child, but he was born with a lip and pallet deformity. Prince Stefano reconstructed his face.' The woman's face seemed to glow. 'It is a miracle.'

Many miscarriages. Kiki could only imagine the pain. 'That's wonderful, Elise.'

The woman nodded eagerly. 'And his work is not confined to those who know the family. He will repair any child, and do what he can for the damage that affects peoples' lives. He is a great man.'

No wonder Stefano had wanted her exposed to Elise. The woman hero-worshipped him. Kiki would hold judgement until this afternoon, but it seemed Stefano had had many reasons apart from his accident for not contacting her when she'd needed him.

There was so much to learn about him and yet so little time. And he had shared barely anything with her of his life here. She wondered if her exposure to Elise was the most he could do to open up.

By the time they had drunk their tea and eaten the tiny pomegranate cakes a maid had brought the glass doors opened and Stefano strode in. Suddenly the huge apartment seemed smaller.

'Ah, here you are, and I see you've had tea.'

Elise jumped up, wreathed in smiles. 'And cake. Will you join us, Highness?'

He'd changed into less formal dark trousers and an open-necked shirt so she could hopefully assume his royal duties were over.

'No. Thank you.' He glanced at his watch and then at Kiki. 'I hate to rush you, but flights are easier to and from the island the earlier in the day we travel. Air currents become stronger as we go into late afternoon. Are you happy if we leave for the hospital soon?'

Rough air currents on the way home? Excellent. 'Of course.' She tried to sound upbeat. 'Are we flying?'

'No.' He smiled as if he knew it was an act. 'We will be driving across as I wish to give you a brief glimpse of the scenery on the island. But we must get back to the ship as promised.'

Their trip to the other side of the island started with a winding descent from the castle—an exercise in S bends with the cliffs falling away to the side and the sea below. Not dissimilar from being in a helicopter, really.

Stefano drove a little convertible with total disregard for the precipice, and despite a few gasps on the whole Kiki knew she was safe. Strange.

'I hope this isn't where you had your accident?'

He laughed. 'Nothing so impressive. I hit a cow on the way to the hospital.'

At the bottom of their descent they drove parallel to the beach, and Stefano pointed out the famous race track where the Prince's Cup would be held the following week. She remembered what Ginger had said. 'A nurse on the ship says you have quite a social event with your race.'

He smiled. 'It is popular with the sophisticated traveller and with philanthropists, and we raise more than enough money to cover the hospital's costs for that year as well as for several health research projects. Last year we raised money for a gynaecological wing which opens in a few days.'

'So it's not just a party?' She liked that.

He shook his head. Twice. 'It is a week of tedious social engagements which I would prefer not to have to attend, but the good it achieves makes me appreciate the generosity of those who come.'

'Poor sad Prince. So you don't have any fun?'

He flashed a grin at her. 'Sometimes. The race is fun. If you would consider joining me I think I could have more fun?'

She'd bet he would. 'While you make a fortune?'

'That too.'

Not a sensible idea. 'Sorry. I'm a working girl.'

He flashed another grin at her. 'I thought you might say that.'

There was something in his voice that made her frown, but just then they rounded a bend and turned away from the sea. Now they drove through rolling vistas of olive groves with grey-green leaves that glittered like stars in the sunlight and stretched away to the base of the mountain and a third of the way up its sides.

'We grow only three varieties of olive here and Aspelicus is famous for the gourmet oil it produces. One of my ancestors proclaimed that every family must plant three olive trees a year. We have many thousands of them now.'

'So when do you pick the olives?'

'We harvest in November. It is all done by hand.' She raised her eyebrows, and he laughed. 'I admit. Not *my* hand.'

'But it doesn't hurt to have the Royal Seal on the bottle?'

He grinned. 'Not at all.'

The largest village, though really it seemed almost

like a city, was clustered above the last of the olives and clung to the southern side of the mountain, its red-tiled houses and larger official buildings secured to the rock with Aspelican determination.

She could see the spires of several large churches, and the main belltower of a cathedral soared above the rooftops.

'I love the narrow stone streets. I'll bet the roads are cobbled and cool in the summer up there.'

He glanced where she pointed. 'If you come back I will show you. It is serene and very special. Most families go back hundreds of years.'

'And yours a thousand?' She was teasing him, but she was beginning to see that he had a heritage he was responsible for.

He tapped his forehead. 'Elise has been giving lessons again.'

As if he hadn't known she would. 'Wasn't that the idea?'

He shrugged innocently, and she had to smile when he said, 'I wouldn't dream of boring you.'

'You knew you wouldn't.'

The rapport between them was undeniable, and Kiki could easily have pretended he'd never been away. There was danger in that. Real danger. Because it wasn't true. He *had* gone away, and left her to face the worst time in her life alone. The sparkle seemed to drain from the day.

'Why am I here, Stefano?'

Stefano sighed. He could not but be aware that there was a distance between them that might never be breached, and still he was not sure how to repair the damage. All he knew was that he wanted back his rapport with Kiki. That after months of feeling flat suddenly he was alive again.

'When I saw you I had an idea.' He shrugged and the movement tightened his hands on the wheel. 'A thought to show you my work. Perhaps for you to consider a change in your medical direction. Even to consider coming here and working with me for a time.'

She shouldn't have been surprised. He'd already said they should spend more time together. So he'd been plotting to entice her to his island with the carrot of working with him in surgery...

Unfortunately the idea was attractive, because the tiny fragment of surgery she'd seen him perform in Sydney had been incredible. And she knew he was a good teacher. Further evidence had been in his direction of Wilhelm only yesterday.

To have the opportunity to watch and learn from such a surgeon would be the dream of many a young doctor looking to expand her skills.

But those other doctors wouldn't be as fatally attracted to Stefano as she'd been once before, and she didn't trust him. She knew, fatalistically, that if she moved here and spent time with Stefano he would ensure she become more than an associate. She would become the Prince's temporary mistress.

She must have been silent for an extended time, because the car slowed and she could feel his gaze on her.

'Do not concern yourself. This discussion is for another day. Enjoy the moment without strain. Let me show you first. Not obliged or pressured to consider anything you do not wish to do. It is my foolish pride that wants to show you my work.'

He shrugged. 'Of course I do not like the idea of

you going off to live your life without the chance of at least sharing my own dreams with you.'

Life. Dreams. Chance. All dangerous words for Kiki. Empty words. What was he trying to do?

'Why me?' And how was she going to quiet her unsettled thoughts now that he had spoken?

His attention returned to the road. 'Why anything?'

He was giving nothing else away.

Their snaked their way up a final hill and against the backdrop of more marching rows of olives a modern building sprawled elegantly over several acres, two-storeyed, and painted olive-green to blend into the countryside.

The closer they drove the more attractive it became. Now Kiki could see vine-covered verandas running around both floors, and the windows winked with white wooden shutters latched back against the olive walls.

'It's so pretty.' Gorgeous, really.

'My mother's design.' Pride was unmistakable in the gesture of his hand and in his voice.

'You miss her?'

'Very much.' He kept his eyes on the road. 'She was the voice of reason and the one who did not hesitate to laugh at me if I became too serious. Perhaps that is why I find you a breath of fresh air.' He looked away. 'But then she could forgive me if I made a mistake.'

He looked thoughtful for a moment, shrugged and went on.

'She could not change my father, for he was trained differently, but she influenced me greatly with her humanity and sense of fairness.'

This unexpected insight into Stefano as a very young man touched her deeply. 'When did she die?'

He hesitated, as if it was physically difficult to talk about himself. 'When I was a teenager. An unexpected aneurism. Before I began medical school.'

So he had lost his mother around the same age as she had. She knew that feeling. The devastation, the aching void in the family, the feeling of betrayal at being left an orphan. 'I lost both my parents in a car accident.'

He looked at her. 'I am sorry. I did not ask enough about you in Sydney.'

She grimaced to herself. 'No, you didn't. But I understand your loss.' And there had been little time between work and bed for conversation. 'I had my sisters and Nick to look after me.' To look after the nuisance youngest sister. Though to be fair Nick had never treated her like that.

'But it is not the same, eh?'

'No.'

But this was not what she needed to think about as her baby's birthday came closer, and she pulled her mind away from the fact that she'd finally felt complete at the thought of being a mother. That too she had lost. As she would Stefano when the time came— a huge reason not to risk losing her heart to this man again. She was sick of loss.

But Stefano's past? It was the last thing Kiki had expected. A royal tragedy—the loss of a mother he adored. Kiki began to wonder about the man who ruled this little principality—Stefano's father. A man who didn't forgive easily. Who'd been brought up differently from someone with a sense of humour, perhaps?

It made her wonder what sort of life it had been for

the young Stefano and his brother after their mother died. How had his father reacted to her death? How had these events moulded the man she'd thought she'd known?

But they had arrived.

CHAPTER SEVEN

STEFANO STOPPED THE car and vaulted over his door to come round to hers. Flamboyantly he opened it and held out his hand. 'Come. Let me show you my work.'

Kiki looked at his fingers, outstretched, waiting, and handed him her handbag. Especially vulnerable after the recent disclosures, now was not the time to ler herself hold his hand. But scrambling from a low-slung sports car was a little more difficult than climbing down from the helicopter. She achieved it, although not with elegance, and eventually stood beside him. It would have been easier to take his hand. She ignored the tilt to his mouth and allowed him to lead the way.

The foyer of the hospital was bright and airy, with serene watercolour seascapes and lush potted greenery. The receptionist appeared and bowed, and Kiki was reminded that this man was accorded deference. But not from her. He seemed to cope with that remarkably well, really.

They were met by an auburn-haired woman with bright green spectacles perched on a snub nose. She had a stethoscope poking from the pocket of her white coat. 'Your Highness. Welcome.'

'Ah, Dr Herore, I hope you are well?'

'Yes, thank you.'

He gestured to Kiki, who stood quietly by his side. 'This is Dr Fender.'

Kiki and the young doctor shook hands, and she could tell the woman was wildly curious about her, in a nice way, and that made it easy to smile.

Stefano strode forward and they hurried to catch up. His whole demeanour had changed again and it was easy to see he loved his work. 'How are my patients today?'

'Jerome has been very silly and picked at his stitches. He will not listen to me, but perhaps now you are here…'

'We will start there.' He turned to Kiki. 'Jerome is five.' He slanted a glance at her. 'An orphan, caught in a bomb blast. I have been reconstructing his face and chest. He has been very brave but is quite the mischief.'

They walked the length of the corridor and turned into another wing. The wooden floors glowed with the deep red of cedar and Kiki wondered where they'd sourced these building materials on an island this size. It was a warm alternative to the marble everywhere else.

In the children's ward teddy bears, bright red cars and happy circus animals adorned the walls. With his back to them, a little boy was hunched over a red fire engine. By the set of his shoulders he wasn't happy.

Stefano stopped and tilted his head at the solemn figure. 'Jerome, what is this I hear?'

The child turned and even in the shadows his surly face lit up when he saw Stefano. But the ravages of war were still apparent in the criss-cross of tiny sutures that mapped his mouth and neck as he jumped to his feet and limped towards them in his striped pyjamas.

'Papa,' he lisped in broken English, and Dr Herore bent down and hushed him.

'You must not call His Highness this.'

'All is well, Dr Herore. Until he finds his new family I may be his papa. And how are you, my son? What is this I hear of scratching sutures?'

The little boy hung his head and Stefano tilted his chin with one gentle finger.

'No more of this. My good work and that of Dr Herore needs to be carefully nurtured. Like the plant you care for me. How *is* my plant?'

The boy looked up with worship and reached for Stefano's hand. 'See the plant,' he said, and Stefano allowed himself to be dragged towards the window. 'It goes well, and when it is strong I too will be strong.'

'This I believe—and see how pretty it is?' They both gazed at the robust olive seedling in a red pot. 'I wish this for you, too, so you must promise not to scratch your sutures.'

'I will not.'

'Good. Now, climb to your bed and I will wash my hands. This is my friend Kiki. She is a doctor too, and I would like to lift the bandages on your chest and show her how well you are healing. If that is all right with you?'

'Okay.' It seemed nothing could faze his good humour now that his hero was here.

Kiki could barely restrain her smile. There was so much pleasure to be had from their conversation, but even in short acquaintance she could tell Jerome was far too serious to laugh at. She had not expected Stefano's rapport with children. But then he had been good with Mikey too. It made her wonder why he had left having a family so late when he would obviously be a splendid father. The smile slipped from her face and she glanced away from the little boy.

'Perhaps we will be able to leave the bandages down today and the dressing will not annoy you so much?' Stefano looked at Dr Herore.

She crossed her fingers and said softly while the boy's back was turned, 'It would help. He has been very patient, but the bandage is chafing him and he will not let us touch it.'

When Stefano had donned the gloves that Dr Herore had laid open a nurse wheeled in a trolley with dressing equipment.

Stefano spoke to Kiki but his words were for Jerome even though he didn't look at the boy. 'It makes me sad when Jerome does not let my fellow doctors and nurses look at his wound, because when I telephone for his progress they cannot tell me.'

Jerome shifted guiltily on the bed, but Stefano continued to gaze steadily at Kiki.

'He has been brave and strong since he came here. Now we have repaired his face and neck and used skin grafts for his chest he will be as other boys his age when we have finished.'

'Except I will have learnt your English.' The boy held his head still as he spoke.

'It is not *my* English. We speak it here so that all you children may grow up with two languages at least. Now is the perfect time to learn.'

Jerome shrugged. 'I do not mind.'

Luckily Kiki's giggle drew a smile from the boy and not a frown.

'She's nice, your friend.'

'I think so.' Stefano was engrossed in lifting the edges of the thick dressing carefully. The little boy's fingers clenched on the sheet but he didn't move.

Kiki stepped closer and slid her fingers across the sheet next to his.

Jerome looked up with gritted teeth and tentatively reached out and held onto her fingers as if to draw strength. Kiki's eyes stung as she studied the brave little face and saw his sheer determination to be good. When she glanced up she saw Stefano had stopped his easing of the bandages and was watching her.

'Did I not say he was brave? But we will count to five—' he wagged his fingers at Jerome '—in English, before we start so that he can be brave again.'

Gradually the extent of the chest wound was exposed, and Kiki had to fight not to dig her own nails into the sheet. Everywhere across the boy's sunken chest tiny sutures trailed over the livid skin like rows of tiny ants, pulling together what must have been an almost mortal wound.

'Ah. It heals well. Your big heart is safe again.' The wound was clean and dry, and the graft site looked well fixed. 'Dr Herore will check the donor site later today, when you have had a break from people disturbing your wounds but you are on the mend, my brave friend.'

When it was done Jerome let go of Kiki's fingers as if he'd never needed them and turned his worshipping eyes to his hero. 'That is good.' Then he broke into Lebanese.

To her surprise Stefano answered him fluently and the conversation flowed over her head.

While Stefano spoke with Jerome, Kiki was drawn to a cot in the corner of the room, where a dark-haired little girl with a bandaged hand heavily disguised by white crêpe sat quietly. The little girl turned big, mournful eyes to Kiki and did not return Kiki's tentative smile.

'And what is your name, little one?'

Dr Herore spoke from behind her shoulder. 'Her name is Sheba and she is from the nearest village. Her mother comes daily. Sheba's fingers were almost amputated in an accident, Prince Stefano has managed to reattach, and we have great hopes she will regain full use.'

'She seems heavily bandaged.'

'This one we cannot stop from pulling at her wound, so it needs to be well out of her way. We are still worried it may become infected.'

Just then a small-boned woman came into the room. Until she turned sideways to curtsey to Stefano Kiki didn't realise she was heavily pregnant.

'Ah, here comes mama now. *Bongiorno*, Rosa.'

The woman was panting a little as she arrived, and Kiki wondered if she was in some pain. Her face seemed especially strained, even though she smiled at Dr Herore.

'*Ciao*, Dr Herore. How is my little Sheba today?'

They all looked at the little girl standing on tiptoes in her cot, reaching out for her mother, and such was the anguish on her little face Kiki could barely watch.

'She misses you badly.'

'*Si.*' Rosa brushed away her own tears, heaved the

little girl into her arms to comfort her and was almost
strangled by the tightness of her daughter's grip.

Dr Herore dropped a hand on Rosa's shoulder. 'A
few more days, until the risk of infection is gone, and
she will be able to go home.'

'I know. She is so lucky to come here. And soon my
new baby will be born and Sheba will be home.'

Stefano crossed the room and joined the conversation. 'Take care, Rosa. You are rushing too much at
the end of your pregnancy. You must be well for this
little one too.'

'Yes, Your Highness.' Rosa looked totally overwhelmed by Stefano and Kiki glanced at him, confused by the many facets of this man she had thought
special but still a man.

The silence became a little awkward and Stefano
settled it for everyone. 'Time passes.'

Though Kiki felt he was very aware he was disturbing the mother's time. He nodded kindly, brushed
the shiny hair of little Sheba, and placed his hand on
Kiki's arm.

'Come, before we leave I will show you the viewing
window into our theatres. I am very proud of them.'

As they left Kiki glanced back at the children, at
the warmth they all showed towards Stefano. As the
distance increased she could just make out the mother
and child locked in an embrace.

'How did Sheba hurt her hand?'

'A dog attacked her—thus the risk of infection has
been very great. She has many intermittent antibiotics
so she cannot go home yet, which is hard. Her mother
will not miss a day and walks four miles to see her.'

'Can't you send a car to bring her?'

He smiled at her censure. Shook his head at the idea of doing so. 'I offered and she declined. I will get Dr Herore to ask again. But I must be careful of the old ways of the village.'

'The children love you.'

He shook his head. 'They are away from their families. It is easy to grow attached to an adult they think will keep them safe.'

She didn't think that was it at all.

They left the children's ward behind and turned another corner to climb a tiny spiral staircase with intricate ironwork. The steps were narrow, and looked incredibly old and frail for a new building.

Stefano saw her hesitate. 'As you see, these stairs have been restored. They are safe.'

'Okay. I believe you.' She was beginning to understand that Stefano took his responsibilities very seriously. And he didn't know he should have felt responsible for *her*.

He ran his fingers up the iron handrail and there was something so gentle and reverent in the way he touched the cold steel she couldn't help the memory of other times when she had watched his hands—on her...

When he spoke she almost stumbled, jerked from the past, and he put out his hand to steady her.

Luckily it was only for a moment, and his conversation remained on the steps. 'They are from a section of the castle that crumbled in a landslide and had become dangerous. I had them transplanted to this spot. They are beautiful, are they not?'

She ran her hand gently over the balustrade. 'I've always wanted a spiral staircase.'

He smiled down at her. 'Come work for me and I could call it the Kiki Stairwell.'

So now he would name a staircase after her? Tempting, but… 'You never give up. I'm sure the others who spend so much time here would not be happy with such favour.'

He shrugged. 'It is my hospital. I do as I wish.'

That was the man she knew was under there. 'How disagreeable.'

He stiffened, searched her expression, and then relaxed at the amusement on Kiki's face. 'Perhaps, sometimes, I am. Even need to be.' It was a fact—not an apology.

They reached the top of the stairs and turned onto a landing with windows on both sides of a narrow corridor. The outward-facing window opened over the roof and the lawns, and the inward-facing windows gave a superb view of a pristine operating theatre. Even from here Kiki could tell Stefano had every latest device for his patients, for comfort, and for the surgeon's expertise.

She couldn't help but imagine working there. Working with him. 'Wow. It's fabulous.'

Stefano looked quietly pleased by her response. 'I knew you would appreciate the promise of facilities like these.' He turned and his face grew more serious. 'Even in the few days I saw you at your work in Sydney, barely trained in operating theatre techniques, you had the potential to be a great surgeon. Yet I find you on a pleasure ship?'

'And you.' She was flippant. 'Ironic isn't it?' *Don't spoil the day*, she thought. But they'd always be skirting the edge of this discussion.

'So why did this irony occur?' Stefano watched her. He could see she would choose not to enlighten him and he stamped back his impatience.

She shrugged. 'Things happen. Life throws you something you don't expect and your path changes.'

He wished she would tell him something he didn't know. 'And what changed *your* path, Kiki. Or who?'

She turned her back. Stepped closer to the next window. 'So, tell me about the type of operations you have here. Is this the only OR you have?'

'*Bah!* You are like a clam.' She was the most frustrating woman. He would never have believed it before.

She shrugged. 'And you are used to getting your own way. Not this time.'

He looked at her. Her back was towards him. None of his people would have dared to turn their backs on him. It did not seem at all difficult forKiki to do so. But he would not have her different. He revelled in the difference.

'So we continue the dance.' *Bah* again.

Then he shrugged and went on as if the conversation had never happened. He saw the slight loosening of her shoulders. So she was more tense than she appeared. He would watch for that sign again.

'Operating theatres. We have two others—though one is really only used in emergencies.'

She turned to face him. 'What emergencies do you have?'

'Most often the sudden influx of more than one patient. It is word of mouth. I have a representative in most medical facilities in trouble spots where children are at risk. They contact my team and when information is gathered they can phone me any time. We discuss if the child or children will be strong enough to withstand the journey. To remove a child from all they know is no light matter.'

She could certainly see that. 'Of course not. So who brings them?'

Good. She was deeply interested. He relaxed a little as he let her into his world. The memories of many retrievals coloured his response.

'I have a team who fly in and out when we hear of a case that would benefit greatly from our intervention. There is also a political team who work with governments and organise extradition, and a medical team that goes in on the ground to source the patient from whatever hospital they are in and stabilise for transport.'

'Sounds efficient.'

They were paid to be efficient. 'Most times. Before they retrieve, my political team endeavours to trace parents and relatives, if we can find them alive, so they know the child has survived and is being cared for. We always leave a point of contact.'

He watched her lean her nose against the glass, and not for the first time today he wanted to turn her cheek his way and kiss those stubborn lips of hers.

'Your organisation sounds amazing, but still, a medical crisis for a child… Losing their families… The children must be terrified.'

'I am very aware of that.' Something crossed his face that made her look more closely at him, but he turned away and took a step closer to the viewing window, so that all she could see was his profile. *Back off, I'm royalty*, was stamped all over it.

It was his turn to use the window to escape. 'As you

see, the other theatres are along here—but perhaps we should go. It is getting late.'

She'd said something to upset him. The mood had changed, and it seemed there was nothing she could do about that now, as he marched her along corridors towards the entrance. In the distance she could see the children's ward, and she wished she could revisit again just for a short time.

But he had moved on more than physically. 'I have asked the helicopter to meet us here. We'll fly back to the palace for lunch—there is a group of people I must meet with—then leave for the ship straight after.'

As they took off and soared across the tops of the olive groves it seemed surreal that her pilot was a prince, and she was the reason they were flying across these paddocks. How did she feel about that? Honoured? Chuffed? Excited? Certainly not oblivious.

Well, she wouldn't be human if she didn't feel a little bit special. But it was only one day. She'd just have to be careful to protect herself, because her senses were going into overload with all this care he was taking of her.

She'd enjoyed morning tea in the intimacy of the family apartments, and she hoped, if she was lucky, lunch would be similar, only with Stefano present.

How wrong could she be?

Lunch was served in the formal section of the palace, and she could barely see him at the head of the table, let alone need to worry about accidentally touching him. It seemed her escort—what a joke—was in great demand, judging by the procession of dignitaries that kept interrupting any attempt on his part to address his food.

There'd been a brief flurry of attention when everyone in the room had looked at her as she had been introduced to his father—a shorter version of Stefano, with bushy white eyebrows and scarily piercing blue eyes—and her composure had taken a beating as the older man had stared right through her.

Stefano had moved her on and then handed her over to Elise again, so she'd felt transformed back into parcel mode, and the island's hero had disappeared even faster than before. She'd begun to have an inkling as to how busy his life was when he was home and just what might have happened to thoughts of her when he went away.

But that still hadn't prepared her for lunch.

To say the lunch was formal was an extreme understatement.

She'd half expected a servant to bring in a whole pig, complete with apple in mouth, but they didn't. Not that they didn't have the silver serving dishes and a multitude of crystal glasses down pat. And this was *lunch*. About as intimate as a hotdog at a football game.

The woman beside her constantly complained about how far down the table she was while the tall, good-looking man on her other side quivered with mischief. There was something about him that reminded her of Miko, the charmer of the ship. There was no decision on who she'd rather talk to.

She held out her hand. 'My name is Kiki Fender. A pleasure to meet you.'

He took her hand in his with studied gallantry. '*Bon-*

giorno, signorina. Franco Tollini.' Of course he raised it to his lips instead of shaking it.

His kiss lingered on her fingers. Kiki kept her grin behind her lips but unfortunately for the first time since she'd sat down managed to catch Stefano's eye. How amusing—for her, at least. The Prince seemed less than happy. She turned back to her companion, who had no intention of letting this opportunity go by.

Franco reluctantly gave back her hand. 'I am part of the Prince's team. We transfer the children home to their parents when they are well enough to return.'

'So do you have a medical background, as well, Franco?'

'*Si*. Dr Tollini.' He shrugged with self-deprecation. 'I am a specialist in rehabilitation, but since coming here I have been performing some surgery.'

'Ah. The hospital. You obviously enjoy your work.'

He smiled, and thankfully Kiki could see it wasn't just in appreciation of her. He did love his work.

'The children are incredible. And it is my job to take them back to their families after they heal and help them settle.'

She couldn't help but think of Jerome. 'What if their parents are not there?'

His dark eyes flashed with fervour. 'Then they are adopted into families that will take very good care of them. Our mission is not to lose them entirely. We ensure their schoolwork is well catered for, and more often than not they will have better learning when they return, with opportunities for further study provided if they wish.'

Why hadn't she heard more about this place? 'It seems a fabulous cause.'

Earnestness shone from Franco's eyes. 'Prince Stefano is a great humanitarian and a great surgeon.'

Another fan. She was surrounded by them. 'I have heard the Prince is also a good teacher.'

'Spare my blushes, Kiki.'

They both looked up as Stefano sat elegantly down on her other side, like an unhurried lion settling to watch his prey. Goodness knew what he'd done with the person who'd been there a moment ago, Kiki thought, and had a sudden vision of the woman being thrown into a dungeon by Stefano merely because he'd wanted her seat.

'Hello there, Franco.'

'Your Highness.' Strangely, with Stefano now beside her, Franco seemed to shrink and become a little less boldly defined.Again Kiki realised the Stefano she'd thought she'd known was a totally different person when in his own pride. There was that lion analogy again. She could almost see his aura of power, which grew more apparent despite the gentleness of his tone.

Stefano went on conversationally. 'I've just been showing Dr Fender over the hospital.'

Franco looked at her, and then at the Prince. He swallowed. 'I was just telling…' he paused nervously '…Dr Fender, about our work. She has not had a chance to mention she knows you or that she's seen the hospital.'

'How remiss of her.'

Kiki had had enough of this. She turned to Stefano. 'And how unfortunate that you interrupted our conversation.'

His eyes flared but his voice remained even. 'My apologies. But the helicopter awaits and we must return—or should we be delayed until tomorrow?' He let the question hang.

Kiki blinked, decided she needed to be on the ship, and pushed back her chair. One of the waiters nearly broke his leg, trying to get to her to help, but he was still too slow for Stefano. The Prince assisted her sardonically.

The sooner she left here and returned to the real world, the sooner her head could try to sort out the hundreds of different messages she was getting today.

'Goodbye, Franco. Nice meeting you.' Deliberately she held out her hand, quite sure Franco wouldn't kiss it this time, with Stefano watching.

She was right.

Franco also stood. 'Goodbye, Dr Fender.' He bowed deeply. 'Your Highness.'

'You were really obnoxious.'

Stefano nodded and smiled as the dignitaries bowed as they departed. He ignored the hiss from Kiki beside him and kept her hand firmly in his. To hell with what the gossips said.

It had been a very unusual day. He supposed he should really try and curb his desire to run through any man who spoke to Kiki, let alone those who actually kissed her hand, but he wasn't sure it was worth the effort.

He was beginning to understand the pirate tendencies of his ancestors when they'd captured women and dragged them off. His mother would have been horrified. Then he smiled and remembered something she had once said to him about his father's courtship.

Perhaps his mama would not have been so horrified after all.

When they reached the helicopter he waved the pilot into the front with his man and climbed into the back with Kiki.

When she said, 'I think I'll sit in the front...' he laughed out loud and helped her fasten her seat belt.

When he looked again at her face she was shaking her head. The struggle on her face suddenly gave way and she smiled too.

They grinned at each other, and his relief was a warning about how much this woman's good opinion mattered to him. That and having his arms around her. He'd been fantasising about that all day. Not his usual *modus operandi*. It would be better if he kept Kiki in his bed—that way she would not mess with his head, just his skin. Even at this brief thought his body stirred.

But his prestige would suffer if others heard the way she spoke to him. He really needed to do something about that, but he wasn't sure what. He had a feeling that a direct order would give her the excuse to walk away.

She straightened her face and pretended to frown at him. 'I'm not happy with you.'

He inclined his head and threw caution to the wind rushing by outside the helicopter. 'And there are things I need to discuss about *your* behaviour. Perhaps we could examine this over dinner. Privately. Say seven? My suite.'

'Six-thirty, if you don't mind. I work tomorrow. And the restaurant will be fine.'

Kiki wondered if she'd gone too far. She'd been very surprised when Stefano had decided against piloting their way back to the ship, and disappointed she wasn't going to have the cooling-off period she needed to recover from his grabbing her hand like that and marching her onto the helicopter.

It had certainly surprised a few people—not least her.

The problem was as soon as he'd touched her she'd been captive, and it had nothing to do with force. She glanced down at her fingers in her lap. She wouldn't have been surprised if her hand glowed like one of those luminous fish in the deepest depths of the ocean they were flying over right now. It felt irradiated with his touch, still warm from his warmth, and she was still subdued by the leashed power she had felt.

She wriggled her fingers until his hand came in over hers and stilled them. She glanced up and saw the devilish gleam in his eyes grow. *He knew.* Her face flamed and she pulled her hand away.

Stefano smiled. 'You may choose the restaurant this time.' He turned to look out of the window.

They landed back at the airport without too many of the bumpy updrafts Stefano had mentioned. There were a few minutes' delay while they waited for the pilot to give them the all-clear to alight, and then their transfer by car back to the wharf beside the ship took no time.

Kiki could feel herself tense as she waited for the vehicle to stop. Suddenly everything was awkward, overwhelming—the gulf between them, the hundreds of different examples of how Stefano's life and upbringing were so different from hers. She was a fool to think anything could come of falling in love with this man. She should never have agreed to dine with him.

'Thank you, Your Highness, for an interesting day. Excuse me if I rush off. I must check in with my colleagues.'

He leaned towards her and spoke over the noise of the ship's loudspeakers. 'Liar.'

She forgot her recent revelation and glared back at him. 'Bully.'

His eyebrows rose. 'Two hours' time.'

Thankfully someone opened her door to help her out and she could escape.

For the next two hours Kiki felt as if a huge clock was ticking inside her head. Each tick was louder than the previous one as the hands crept closer to six-thirty. With an hour to go she'd tried and discarded a hundred excuses, each lamer than the last, and in desperation taken herself down to the sick bay to see what was going on there. Nothing. The place was locked and empty.

She declined to ride back up in the lift. It was the hour for pre-dinner drinks, and well-dressed men and women would be crowding the lifts for the next few hours, so she trod the stairs, hoping the exercise might burn off some of the nervous energy she seemed over-endowed with.

Nothing for it but to get dressed and get it over with. The problem was she still didn't know what she wanted.

If she was honest with herself there were many reasons why she would love to go to Aspelicus and work. Not the least that it was time to leave the ship, stretch her brain, learn new skills. But was it time to risk her heart again? And why this week, of all weeks, when her guard was down from a countdown she'd been dreading? Could she keep the distance she knew she'd need when she was feeling so fragile?

CHAPTER EIGHT

WHEN KIKI ARRIVED for dinner, she'd chosen black. The demure effect of her high collar was lost by the keyhole yoke neckline which allowed a glimpse of the swelling valley between her breasts.

Stefano rose smoothly, as did his libido, and one glance at the *maître d'* was enough to keep the man away from her chair.

'You look stunning.' He leaned over her shoulder as she was seated. Along with the subtle scent of spring flowers he always associated with Kiki the view was even more incredible from this angle.

He returned to his seat and looked across at her with a lightness of spirits he wasn't used to.

As he glanced down at the menu he wondered how she did it—lifted him from being immersed in business, too involved in matters of state, too focussed on his patients. She made him remember he was truly a man who deserved a life that was not always lived for others. It was this quality that so intrigued him, tantalised his consciousness, because *with* her he felt unlike he did at any time without her.

They had two days left —not enough to throw caution to the winds, but enough to convince her she needed to join his team. And then he could see if they had a future. Already it was at that stage.

When they had both ordered, and the champagne had been poured, he raised his glass. 'To an interesting day together.'

She bit back a laugh. *Interesting* didn't nearly describe it. 'Great word-choice.' He did make her laugh. *'Salute.'*

He leaned forward. 'So, what did you think of my hospital.'

Kiki felt her shoulders relax a little. He'd started with an easy one. Thank goodness.

She'd spent the last half an hour shoring up her defences. She needed a protective barrier around herself just in case he brought up the fact that she was like soft soap in his hands as soon as he touched her.

The easy stuff first.

'Your hospital is amazing. I love your work and the miracles you create.' *And I see you love children.* But she didn't say it. Couldn't say it. She just felt the gaping hole and smoothed it over before it could cloud her mind.

He smiled, and her heart ached while she smiled back. It wasn't fair. Why had she crossed paths with a man it would be so hard to forget?

He leaned towards her. His intense gaze captured her as easily as if he'd caught her physically, yet her fingers were tucked safely in her lap.

'And if I offered you a position there? On a surgical term, learning what I could teach you? Would you be interested?'

'Is that what you are offering?' Because she knew

without a doubt that if she became his mistress again she would lose herself. One day she would regret it.

And she worked hard, believed in the good she could do, and deserved more self-respect than choosing that life for herself.

'It is a job offer. Yes. I believe so.'

'Do you?' She shook her head. 'If it was a stand-alone package, just that position, it would be hard to refuse.' These were dangerous waters and she saw the flare of triumph in his eyes. *Not so fast, buddy.*

She read his fierce intelligence, searching between her words, sifting for weakness, assessing his own strengths.

He took a sip from his glass and set it down. 'And what did you think of the palace?'

The palace. She thought of his father's cold eyes. The long formal rooms. Her own feeling of insignificance and his vast importance. Not a comfortable place. 'Your palace is very beautiful.' Now to the more difficult part. 'But I wouldn't want to live there.'

'So where *would* you live?'

'In the village. A walk across the fields would be a delight after a hard day in the OR. I could practise my Italian, or French, or whatever language it is they speak up there.'

'Italian.' He sat back with a smile. 'So you have at least thought about the position?'

'And its disadvantages.' She didn't delude herself that he would marry her, or even that she wanted to be a princess, watching her husband from the other end of a long, table of dignified guests. But that was far fetched.

He frowned. 'Disadvantages? I see none.'

The entrées arrived. As they ate she changed the

subject. 'Elise said you operated on her son? Was the defect a difficult one?'

'Yes. Full thickness and requiring several operations.'

He explained in detail and drew on the table with his finger, outlining the sections that had required repair. Again he made it easy for her to understand why and how.

She would learn so much, the voice inside her insisted.

'His mother is pleased with his recovery,' she said.

'Elise has had a hard life. She would have loved more children. Though with her husband passed away that will not be possible unless she remarries.'

'I can't imagine her leaving her position. She admires you very much.'

'She has worked for our family since she was a girl. For the last few years she's been my housekeeper and she expects perfection for me.'

Now, *that* brought up an interesting topic. 'She said you must marry before you are forty. Are you feeling the pressure?' Did she really want to know this? In case he thought she was putting herself forward, she hurriedly added, 'I'm sure there are dozens of perfect future princesses out there for you.'

'A few.'

He was watching her and she didn't know where to look. 'So what happens if you don't?'

He shrugged. 'I forfeit my royal inheritance.'

She frowned. He didn't seem too perturbed. 'Might it be hard to live as a subject again?'

He shrugged again. 'I make my own fortune. I spend it on the hospital. I would have more than enough to live on, and I would still be a prince. I could not leave my country for personal satisfaction.'

Her stomach sank and her appetite drifted away. 'So you will marry?'

'Yes.' He smiled, but there was no humour in his eyes. 'My father has several women he approves of.'

She knew one his dad wasn't so keen on. 'Congratulations.'

'Are not in order yet.' He glanced at her plate, seeing the signs that she had eaten all she wanted. 'Dessert?'

'No, thank you.' She folded her napkin and placed it on her side plate.

He lifted the bottle. 'More wine?'

She shook her head and took another sip of the mineral water she'd changed to before the main course.

'Good.' He signalled the waiter. 'Then if you have eaten enough perhaps we could go somewhere more private to finish this discussion?'

Kiki glanced around. The atmosphere was elegant, non-intrusive and discreet. Above all—safe. 'I think not. I'm very happy with the company we are in.'

If he was disappointed he didn't show it. He just waved the waiter away again, as if it was of no matter, then was straight back to the hunt. 'So, what is it you'd want from me if you took this position?'

He had brass, asking that. 'I could ask you the same question.'

'Ladies first.' He gestured with his hand.

'I think not.' She lifted her chin.

'So stubborn.' He glanced away and then back, and she couldn't read the expression on his face. 'So determined not to show me the respect I am used to.'

He was right, but she didn't think she could change.

'I do not intend to offend you. I respect you, but I will not give in to your need for control all the time.' *Because I would lose respect for myself.* And in the end that was all she would have left. *Herself.*

'Well, let me see.' He ran his eyes lingeringly over what he could see of her and smiled. 'The idea of working with you, watching your surgical skills grow, feeding your desire to repair intricately and restore function, to watch you blossom into the surgeon I know you could be—that is enticing.'

Kiki could admit the concept was very attractive. 'And for me also.'

His voice wrapped around her. 'As well, I wish to show you the beauty of my homeland with its depths that you can only begin to imagine. Celebrations like the Prince's Cup, the galas held after the harvest season, the saints' days and the markets...'

He opened his hands and she couldn't help but be enthralled with his passion for his island.

'In my palace are long tunnels from the castle to the sea, works of art nobody views, buildings so old and manuscripts so holy and so fragile even the Pope agrees we do not move them.'

She did appreciate his deep pride, and the responsibility he took with his position, and she was not immune to the honour he spoke of bestowing on her. 'That would be wonderful.'

'And...' He left it hanging.

'Is there more?'

Of course there was more that he wanted. And that was what she was so afraid of.

'Yes. Then there is the heart of it.'

His eyes darkened and his voice took on a quality that made the gooseflesh rise on her arms.

'Then there is the woman who makes me understand the baser instincts of a bygone age. Who makes me remember I am a man not to be trifled with. A woman I burn to protect and long to conquer. I want the lot— and I don't want you staying half an hour from my bed in the village.'

She shivered. It was there. Plain speaking, as she'd asked. There was no doubting his intent—nor the fact that every nerve in her body leaned towards him as he said it. She'd asked for honesty and got it. With a vengeance.

He shrugged his shoulders, as if he'd been discussing the weather. 'But I understand your dilemma.'

Holy Dooley—what could she say to that? 'I don't think you do.'

He tilted his head. 'So tell me.'

Where to start? With her mind blown by the fantasy he had conjured she was starting from way behind. 'I appreciate your honesty...' *Sort of.* She paused. 'And I will try to reply with my own.'

'See...' He smiled and looked at her as if she was a wonder of the world. 'This is why you hold me.'

She shook her head, not willing to be diverted from saying her piece while she had some structure in her head. 'Strictly business. My own residence away, from the castle—preferably in the village, if possible—and set work hours.'

He shook his head. 'I do not find that possible. A single woman living in the village would be prey to gossip and perhaps even harassment.'

He shook his head again, but she ignored him with

a smile. 'The harassment I'm worried about lives in the castle.'

He stared her down, dark eyes full of wicked amusement. 'It is not me you are afraid of, Dr Fender. It is your own base instincts and the fact that we spontaneously combust when we are alone.'

Didn't she know that? 'Exactly. But I did not interrupt you—perhaps you could show me the same courtesy?'

He straightened, only half joking when he said, 'You are speaking to a *prince*.'

But she wouldn't be shut down. Not now. Not by him when so much was at stake. 'And that's why you like me.'

It was Stefano's turn to laugh. 'So what am I to do? See you through the day, toss in my lonely bed at night, only to be exposed to your unreachable womanly wiles again the next day? I think not.'

She spread her hands, borrowing his favourite mannerism. '*Impasse*. Your choice.'

He sat back further and a slow smile crossed his face. 'I will sleep on it. Though I will not sleep.'

She gathered her purse. 'Well, I have to sleep because I have work in the morning. Which reminds me—if you meet my requirements, I would need to give two weeks' notice.'

He glanced away. 'I will see that the cruise line does not suffer, if you leave with me it will be when the cruise ends in two days.'

By the time Kiki made it back to her cabin her knees were shaking. What had she talked herself into? When she'd left this same cabin two hours ago it had never been going to happen and now, after one meal with him,

she was negotiating contracts. *Crazy, foolish woman.*
She needed serious advice.

She didn't know who to turn to. Now would be the
perfect time to talk to Nick, but her brother had his
own life, and anyway they were at sea so her mobile
wouldn't work. She couldn't talk to Ginger because of
the risk of her capturing the scoop of the week for her
ex-boyfriend's gossip column, and Wilhelm, while a
great boss, just wouldn't understand.

But when she went to work the next morning, as the
ship docked in Monte Carlo, everyone already knew.
Because Prince Stefano Mykonides had put in her notice for her and a replacement doctor was arriving tomorrow, when the ship returned to Livorno. So, not
only would tomorrow be the day before the one she
was dreading for emotional reasons, now she would
be out of work and out of her home.

Ginger's eyes were wide with a grudging respect for
Kiki's new notoriety, which didn't help at all.

She looked at Wilhelm and her stomach sank at the
worried expression on his face. She couldn't believe
Stefano had been so arrogantly sure of her decision—
plus so high-handed that he didn't think there would
be repercussions.

It was a classic example of his privileged lack of
thought. How could he not realise this would send her
back the other way?

'It's not true,' she said, conveniently forgetting that
she had already decided to finish work on the ship regardless of Stefano's offer.

Wilhelm patted her on the back. 'Well, the new guy's

coming and your resignation papers have been drawn up without the need for any notice.'

She looked for inspiration or explanation but there was none on Wilhelm's face. 'How could he *do* that?'

Wilhelm shrugged again and rubbed his hands together awkwardly. 'Easily, apparently. It's by order of the cruise line's owner.'

Kiki stared at him and through him, trying to see an answer. 'Can I reverse it?'

Wilhelm sighed. 'Apparently not. I already asked, because I figured it was something like that.'

She could feel incredulous anger building. 'Well, thank you for that.' She could not believe this was happening. At least Will had had some faith in her. 'Of course I wouldn't resign without telling you. I can't believe he's done this. Is he insane?'

Wilhelm rubbed the underside of his jaw. 'No. Just used to power. Owed favours by the owner.'

She needed to get out of this small room before she exploded. This couldn't be happening. 'I'll be right back.'

'You want me to come looking for you if you aren't?' Wilhelm was beginning to get the idea that this man played hard.

She was about to say yes, then thought about the repercussions that didn't just involve her. 'No. I can handle it. You stay out of the firing line. He has just bought more trouble than he knows.'

Kiki fumed all the way up in the elevator. Halfway she briefly wondered if perhaps she should have taken the stairs, to at least try and calm down and heighten the chances that she would act rationally when she arrived.

That thought was vetoed.

As each floor flashed by on the control panel of the lift she couldn't remember ever being this incensed, but the annoyingly persistent voice in her mind was suggesting again that this headlong course of action might not be the wisest one.

Well, to hell with that. He deserved a blast. A quick in and out might not save her job on the ship, but it was going to make her feel a whole lot better.

When the suite door opened she let him have it. 'How dare you—?'

Wrong man. Blast!

She scanned past the shoulders of the bristling man in front of her and spied her prey at the windows of the suite. She took a step, but came up against the surprisingly solid bulk of Stefan's manservant.

'Let her in, Manos.' Stefano's voice was even. 'Then leave.'

Which only served to incense her more.

She threw daggers at him as she waited for the hulk to get out of the way. 'You might want to keep him around for protection.'

'I think not.'

The man hesitated as Kiki swept past, but Stefano waved him on and the door shut silently after him. When she glanced behind her he'd gone. Kiki kept walking until she was a hand's breadth away from him and glared into his face.

'I've upset you.' Stefano watched her with a wariness born of unfamiliarity with this kind of scenario.

'Brilliant deduction, Sherlock.'

He blinked.

'As I was saying—how *dare* you hand in my resignation without my permission?'

He stepped to the side and picked up a half-filled glass of juice. 'Don't you think you are overreacting?'

His voice was mild, but the thread of sudden amusement in it was a torch to Kiki's anger.

'Not yet, I'm not.' There was probably steam coming out of her ears—not that he'd notice.

Unperturbed, he shrugged. 'I saw you were worried about giving the correct amount of notice.' He crossed the room and sat down on the lounge, crossed his legs and looked at enquiringly. 'My cousin owes me favours. I have merely taken the matter out of your hands.'

She spun and stormed across the room until she stood over him. 'Well, I want it back in my hands. And I'm giving you a straight refusal on the offer of a position while I'm at it.'

He remained impassive. 'Don't be foolish. What will you do for a job?'

She lifted her head. 'I have plenty of options.'

That wiped the smile from his face. 'I'm sure you have.'

'What's that supposed to mean?'

He put the glass down and she could tell his temper had slipped a little.

'Whatever you wish.' He rose and took a step towards her, his eyes drilling into her.

Alarm bells started to ring. She needed to get her piece said and go. 'Well, know this, Prince Stefano Mykonides. I'm leaving this ship tomorrow, and I'm *not* going to Aspelicus.'

Then she spun on her heel and got out of there while she still had her clothes on.

The door closed and Stefano stared at it. He should have caught her before she left, because the sex would have been explosively incredible. But in fact he had been in the wrong. Out of line. And to take advantage of her emotion would have made him more culpable, not less.

She was totally correct. He had no right to assume control. *Yet.* Difficult to remember when all his life decisions had needed to be made and he'd gone with them. Most times he chose the correct path. With Kiki it had been one false step after another.

Now he needed to win back her good graces. Because she *was* coming to Aspelicus.

Late that afternoon Stefano waited around the corner beside the lifts. He knew she would be out soon. He could imagine the headlines: *Prince Waits to Pounce on Innocent Doctor!*

The door opened and she walked across the foyer from the hospital to the elevator with a nurse, who pressed the button for the lift.

Kiki's hands were full. At least she hadn't tossed his flowers out, or left them in the waiting room.

It was a two-fold ploy on his part—to apologise in public with flowers, knowing if he made the bunch large enough she would have to take the lift to get them to her room. His plan to throw himself at her mercy would not work if he had to follow her up the stairs.

Amazing how devious he could be when he had to.

He waited until the lift doors began to close and then strode across the distance between them.

'Hold the lift, please.'

He pressed the button for good measure, in case she was quick enough to realise it was him.

He slipped in between them as the doors shut. 'I'm very sorry.'

'You can't buy me with flowers.' Kiki pushed the bouquet towards him but he was way ahead of her.

He took them and handed them straight to Ginger. 'Would you be so good as to hold these?'

Then he turned back to Kiki and lifted her hands in his, squeezed and kissed her fingers.

'Forgive me.'

Her hands and her eyes were cold. 'Done. Now leave me alone.'

The lift slowed. His plan had not met his expectations. Again. Why did that happen with this woman?

'It was a misjudgement on my part. I have withdrawn your resignation.' He hadn't, but he could do it very quickly if need be. He'd hoped for some response, but again she just looked at him coolly and that surprised him.

'I'm sure you haven't.'

How did she know that?

'But don't bother. If the cruise company can do that without my knowledge I don't want to work for them. And if you think you can control my life I certainly don't want to work for *you*. Not everything is under your control, Your Highness.'

The lift stopped.

He watched from the back of the lift as she stepped out, and as she walked away he heard her say, 'I'll see you at the show. Please keep the flowers, Ginger.'

CHAPTER NINE

MONACO WAS A great place to buy a sexy catsuit—even in a thirty-minute dash by tender after work.

The salesgirl had assured her it was latex-free—Kiki didn't want to brush up against Marla and start that whole scenario again—and the blatant sexual statement that she could wear what she wanted, in front of whoever she wanted, would annoy Stefano. She hoped. It was her last chance to do so.

An hour ago it had seemed like a brilliant idea.

The final night crew's pageant always proved popular with the passengers because it was more personal to cheer for their favourite crew member, waiter or cabin person while watching them perform on stage.

Kiki had been dancing at the pageant with Miko for almost four months, so there was little practice needed for their tango session. And this was the last night to end all last nights.

Tonight the theme was the *Lion King*, but any type of animal was acceptable. The skintight silver suit dipped low at the front and, with a sheepdog's tenacity, rounded her breasts up and pointed them in the right direction without the benefit of padding. She hoped it wasn't cold in the auditorium.

Now she was dressed it looked so much worse under fluorescent light, and Kiki laughed with a trace of hysteria. All in all, the suit left nothing to the imagination, she thought as she stared at herself. Maybe she couldn't do this?

But this was her last night aboard. Kiki gulped one last time at herself in the mirror, then stepped out into the corridor.

The first man who saw her whistled.

It was lucky she trusted Miko to look after her, because this suit was designed to say one thing. *Come hither.*

Her shoes clacked down the hallway and she wondered why the heck she hadn't brought a coat. But it was too late now. Maybe it hadn't been such a good idea after all to flaunt herself, but it had seemed the most efficient way of annoying her nemesis for the last time.

Ginger had somehow discovered that Stefano would be in the Captain's box in the auditorium, so he would have a good view of what he couldn't have. That thought straightened her spine.

Unfortunately, once backstage, Kiki had a hard time fielding the ribald comments because Milo had been held up with a disaster in the restaurant. Finally she dragged Wilhelm to stand beside her so he could glower at anyone who dared to raise an eyebrow.

'Not so sure brother Nick would like this outfit, Kiki,' Wilhelm said in his measured way as he looked anywhere but at her.

Kiki felt as if she should pat his arm to comfort him. 'I'm a big girl, Will.'

'I hadn't realised quite how big,' he said, with a rare attempt at humour.

'Wilhelm. Don't you start.'

Thankfully Miko arrived, all suave black panther, and took one appreciative look at her, bowed and kissed her fingers.

'I see we will be dancing for effect, my sweet. I will step up to that challenge.'

This was followed by a ludicrously wicked wink that had Kiki smiling again.

'Well, you only just made it.'

'Such is the drama of my position.' He squeezed her hand, noticed the chill of it, and rubbed her fingers between his own. 'Enjoy your last night. Be Catwoman for me. Hopefully I will not wake up in a dungeon tomorrow.'

Kiki's nervousness receded. Miko always made her feel better. Like a favourite cousin. Funny how she'd never fancied him and yet he was a delight.

'I promise we will have fun.'

She'd never see these people again, would never do anything like this again. She might as well give it everything she had.

She lifted her head and plastered on a smile.

Their turn. The red light came on.

How appropriate for her costume, she thought sardonically as Miko straightened and she put her hand on his arm.

He patted her shaking fingers. 'Good girl. Let's do it.'

Stefano conversed pleasantly with the Captain's wife. It was what he'd been trained to do. He'd promised to attend but he wished the night over, so he could return to his real world and decide on his next strategy for seducing Dr Fender.

His brother and sister-in-law were in very good spirits and had enjoyed their short holiday, and they had all survived without any further dire embarrassments.

The music changed to the unmistakable beat of the tango, and Stefano, like every other male in the auditorium, drew in his breath and held it when Kiki stalked onto the stage.

He heard Theros say, 'Is that the doctor?' but his eyes never moved.

Her ridiculous tail twitched, seductively sinuous and provocative, and the lights caught the skintight shimmer of her perfectly luscious body. Her breasts gleamed high and proud, shimmering with stardust. Stefano's mouth dried.

Mesmerised, he followed every sway and bend, each drift and spin. The woman in silver was heating his blood to boiling point, and never had he wanted her more.

Then he realised every man in the room had their eyes glued on his woman and wanted her too.

The flash of a camera from behind him made him grit his teeth, and he resisted the almost uncontrollable urge to reach back, grab the offending instrument and smash it into a million non-recording pieces. Instead he clenched his hands in his pockets and remembered to breathe, letting the air out slowly and with intent. He repeated the process, as if he would feel better soon. Unfortunately he didn't.

While he could almost admire the grace and precision of the dance, admire the rapport and impeccable timing between male and female, he would have given the crown jewels for it to end. He wanted her covered from head to foot at this moment, as his anger built, preferably bound and in the back of his helicopter heading for home.

How could she flaunt herself so?

As soon as the dance finished, to the most enthusiastic applause of the night, the rest of the cast came on for the final joint farewell and she flaunted herself all over again.

Stefano gritted his teeth as the crew sang their way through the final number. There was thunderous applause and he wondered grimly how much of it was for his little Dr Fender.

Finally he could excuse himself, and with Olympian control he strode to the stage door just as she stepped out in a group.

Thankfully someone had given her a coat. She was laughing as he approached, and that incensed him more, but he was no fool.

Miko was the first to notice his approach. 'Here comes retribution.'

He said it quietly in Kiki's ear but she heard and turned, plastered a smile on her face. 'Did you enjoy the show, Your Highness?'

'Most illuminating.' He smiled at the crowd, moved in next to Kiki, and laced his fingers through hers in a statement nobody could doubt. 'What a naughty suit.'

He stroked her palm with his thumb and her legs almost buckled.

This was not what she'd expected. Battle-ready, Kiki was confused by his soft tone, by the damned weakness she always had when he touched her, and the come down from the adrenalin of the dance. And that thumb, insistently vibrating at the core of her, in tendrils of heat from her palm, was blurring her mind so she couldn't think at all.

Still he hadn't looked at her.

'If you would all excuse us for just a few moments? I'd like to speak to Kiki. We'll catch up.'

She had to hand it to him. He'd asked nicely, but the projection that instant obedience was expected was miraculous—though Miko looked more than a little worried as she handed him back his coat.

How the heck did Stefano do that?

Maybe he didn't even care that she appeared almost naked in some lights. She sneaked a look at his face, saw his eyes and the penny dropped. Might be a good time to run after her friends...

Black pupils filled with sparks and his hand tightened on hers. 'I won't take up much of your time.'

If she could disentangle her hand she'd be able to think.

More people tumbled from the stage entrance and another camera flashed. Stefano swore softly—the first time she'd ever heard him swear—and let go of her hand to remove his jacket.

Kiki's mind began to clear the second they disconnected. She only had these few moments until he put his coat around her shoulders. The reality of the danger switched on like a light in her befuddled brain.

They were on the lowest level open to passengers, one below the gangplank, and there was no way he could get her to his suite unless she got into a lift. So she should be safe if she didn't.

'No lift!' At least she managed to get that out before he captured her hand again.

He nodded. Directed her to the stairs—innocuous enough. Almost as if he knew, his thumb circled her palm again, and her will weakened as a brief lull in the flow of passengers gave them a moment of privacy in the bend of the stairs.

He leaned her back against the wall, captured her chin and kissed her—not with force, he even started gently, though she could feel the tightly leashed control, the simmering emotion as he seduced her with implacable intent. He kissed her thoroughly until she could barely stand, would have followed him blindly over the edge of the ship into the water below.

Then he drew her up to the next level and into a packed but serendipitously waiting lift. It was as if even fate was against her. The whole time his fingers were linked through hers.

Her head began to insist she took note. She looked around and whispered, 'I said no lift.' She tugged on her hand but he didn't let go.

He whispered back. 'If that is the worst I do then you will be lucky.'

The idea was scarily attractive.

'Could you let go of my hand, please?' She said it a little too loudly but it had the desired effect. Everyone turned to look at them and Stefano dropped her fingers like a hot potato. 'Could someone press five, please?'

Her ears burned from the attention but to hell with it. She wasn't going to be monster'd by a royal bully even if she had pulled his tail deliberately. There was very real danger here—and not all of it was coming from him.

The lift stopped on her floor and she alighted without obstruction from Stefano. As the doors shut she refused to look back and took off, with her own tail in her hand, as fast as she could towards the crew's quarters.

The ship docked in Livorno at five a.m. Kiki woke after a restless night with her pillow screwed in a ball under her neck, her sheets twisted and creased and her body aching as if she'd done ten rounds in a boxing match. But worse was the mental exhaustion from duelling with Stefano in her dreams all night.

She crawled into the shower with a whimper, infinitely glad she didn't share her cabin with anyone else.

It was both an anticlimax and a blessing that she wouldn't see Stefano Mykonides and his entourage leave the ship. Because despite her resistance he had invaded her heart again, and now she'd have to re-banish him.

Today was going to be almost as big as tomorrow. She had to say goodbye to colleagues who had been her friends, and she needed to find somewhere to stay tonight with all her luggage.

Then she needed to start forgetting the last week and sorting out a plan of action for work.

When she walked into the medical centre Wilhelm was talking to Ginger, and judging by the amount of gesticulating going on there was a problem.

'You guys okay?'

Ginger had tears streaming down her pale cheeks, Wilhelm was red-faced and angry, and both of them looked at her in varying degrees of distress when she arrived. Kiki felt her stomach sink.

'Tell her.' Wilhelm vibrated with emotion.

Ginger twisted hands that trembled as she turned

to Kiki, but no words came out except a whisper that trailed off. 'I'm sorry…'

Kiki was liking this less by the minute. 'Sorry for what, Ginger?'

Wilhelm couldn't stand it any longer. 'She's sorry she e-mailed your story and a photo to her sleazy gossip columnist ex-boyfriend. You and the Prince will be splashed across every newspaper and magazine that can manage to change their lead article in Italy today.'

Kiki felt the cold seep into her bones. 'What story?'

'That you had an affair with Prince Stefano. That you flew to his island the day before yesterday.' Wilhelm dropped his voice and his eyes, unable to look at her while he broke the worst news. 'And that he didn't come to you when you lost his baby earlier this year.'

Kiki felt sick. And faint. And incredulously angry. 'How did you know about my pregnancy?'

Ginger looked as if she was going to be sick. 'My ex-boyfriend did some digging.'

Kiki's mouth opened and shut several times before words came out. 'And you sent my private life to a newspaper?' She looked at Wilhelm. 'And you knew?'

'No.' He shook his head vehemently. 'Ginger came and told me what she'd done this morning.'

Kiki could barely follow it. All she knew was that the whole sordidly tragic story, the pain and anguish she'd suffered alone, was now up for discussion by any busybody who fancied reading about her. Incomprehensible.

'How could you do that? Why would you do that?'

'I'm so sorry.' Ginger sobbed the words out. 'Last night I'd had too many drinks. Didn't think it through. Josh rang me. Asked for help. He said he was suicidal

and he needed one good story to keep his job. I panicked. I love him, and I was scared he'd do it. So I gave
him the best story I could find.'

'Mine?'

Ginger swallowed and then nodded. 'Yours. But I
didn't know about the baby.'

Kiki sank back into a chair in the waiting room and
shook her head, unable to comprehend just how public
this was. That everyone would know a secret she'd kept
hidden from everyone...most of all Stefano.

'Are you sure they'll publish it? The Mykonides family have a lot of power.' Didn't she know that? With
the thought came the first hint of light. 'Of course they
won't let them publish, and I'm not interesting enough
to write about if his name isn't there.'

Wilhelm spun the computer screen around to show
her. 'It's online already.'

That was when she saw the explicit glory of her catsuit, in full colour, and Stefano holding her hand. She
looked like a call girl.

'That picture...' She put her head in her hands. 'My
family don't know about the baby.' She looked at Wilhelm, but all his sympathy wasn't going to help her
now. 'Nick doesn't know, or my sisters.'

He sighed. 'Then you'd better ring him.'

'I can't.' She shook her head. 'I can't think.' An
image of Stefano flew into her mind and she groaned.
'Stefano... His family... He hates the press.'

Running the gauntlet of the ship as she said goodbye
was nothing compared to the reception the Italian newspaper journalists had planned for her when she stepped
onto the wharf.

The flash of cameras and the surge of the bodies that crowded round her stole the breath from her lungs and she felt herself sway with the onslaught.

A car screeched to a halt.

'Enough!'

One voice, a whiplash of command, and four body-guards, hastily shielding a central figure. The crowd parted and fell silent in shock as Stefano strode forward, dropped his arm protectively around her shoulders and swept her back to his car. Her luggage was quickly packed into a second car by Stefano's man-servant.

As she slid along the back seat the flash as the first photographer recovered ignited others, and the din returned full force as Stefano slid in behind her.

The door shut and both vehicles pulled away. The guards followed behind as Kiki huddled in the corner of the seat, shaking, tears thick in her throat as she tried to regain her composure in a world that had suddenly gone mad.

She supposed she should be thankful he'd come, but she had no idea what to say to him. Where to start. What he thought. Her head still spun from the ramifications of such a private airing of her deepest pain. Many women had suffered such a loss but it hurt even more to expose it publicly. Not just the memory of the physical, the cramps and the loss of control, but emotionally it had been traumatic. And now the world was privy to that pain.

Stefano could barely see straight, barely think as he struggled with a feeling of betrayal greater than anything he had ever experienced before. This did not happen to him. He was careful. In control. Master of his own fate and no one else's—because his goal in life was never to be responsible for someone else's downfall again.

But control had been taken from him. This news had been waiting for him as soon as he woke.

His office had gone into disaster mode. His security staff had arranged a different departure point for himself, Theros and Marla from the ship, to avoid the inevitable press, and he had seen them to the airport and discreet safety. But he'd had to return for Kiki, though he wondered bitterly if she deserved it.

All this because he had terminated her employment. It was a smallness he hadn't expected. Fool that he was. He had been told many times, and even in the last few days by his father, that he should stay within the circle of people who understood the rules. And he had defended her.

Now all the world knew she had been pregnant. *His* child. Even when he had been in hospital she would have been able to reach him. His child had died at the time when he too had almost died. Another painful situation out of his control.

His anger bubbled and boiled. Or had it really been his child? Had there been any child at all?

He sifted through what he knew, what had been written, and tried to discern what was truth and what was fiction even as she who had caused this furore shivered beside him. He would find out. He would keep her close until this all died down and she could not spread more lies about him.

The hardest part was the fact that he had always been the one to protect his family from his brother's many scrapes. His way for making up the past, perhaps. By being the son his father wanted and Theros could not be.

Because of *him*.

But this—this was all his doing, and the woman beside him. They had brought shame to the royal house. Now he needed to be strong. Not weak. He repeated it in his mind. *Show strength not weakness.* The plan of action he had decided on was not the answer, but perhaps it would buy him time and stop the damage to his family until the truth could be ascertained.

Kiki could feel tension vibrating from the man beside her, emanating in waves, like a radioactive leak from a damaged core. Well, she guessed she had pierced his protective shell with the last news he'd expected.

Stefano's voice, coldly formal, as if he were talking to a bare acquaintance he disliked intensely, made Kiki feel even more alone.

'It seems you must come to Aspelicus after all. You will be safe there until all this dies down. The rest we will discuss later, when I can be sure I will not do something I regret.'

That stiffened her spine. As if *she* didn't have regrets. As if *she* had orchestrated the most public airing of her grief. Grief he hadn't even been there to share.

'Oh, it's all about *you*? Typical.'

He shot her a look of loathing and she returned it with interest. 'I am not informed. Yet you tell a newspaper.'

So that was what he thought. Again, typical.

'You think I would share my pain so publicly?' She turned her head and stared at the swiftly passing streets. 'You really don't know me at all, do you?'

She couldn't believe he thought that. But then again why wouldn't he? It was all about him.

Now she was on her way to Aspelicus and too emotionally drained to fight it. Not what she would have believed possible less than twelve hours ago. The way she felt at this moment he could drop her off on the moon and she wouldn't care. In another world she would be waiting with bated breath for her labour to start. For her baby to be born. Instead she was the instigator of an injustice to him.

She just wanted to hide. And cry. But she wouldn't give him the satisfaction. Instead she stared unseeingly out of the window as they turned into the airport and drove onto the tarmac.

Before they got out he had one last thing to say. 'Your pregnancy. Was it really my child?'

Kiki turned her head and stared at this man she'd thought she knew, looked at him with such disgust he flinched.

At last he had the grace to say, 'I apologise.'

But it was too late. Of course he would think that. How could she have ever thought she loved him?

'Too damn late. It will never be unsaid.'

His implacable face stared at her. 'So when were you going to tell me you were pregnant?'

She could do cold. She should be able to, because she felt as if her heart had frozen over like those lakes in Switzerland she'd always wanted to see. Never more than at this moment.

'When you came back. But you didn't. So I tried to phone. But even then I didn't get the chance.'

Her car door was opened from the outside and the helicopter looked almost reassuringly familiar. It was funny how things could change in so short a time, and she was glad when he handed her coldly into the rear of the aircraft and climbed into the pilot's seat himself. At least she wouldn't have to sit next to his smouldering disapproval for the next hour.

Their ascent and the flight were a blur as her mind fought the paralysis this morning had left her with. It seemed only a short time later that they were landing on the forecourt of the palace, and she lifted listless eyes to the gathering that waited for them.

Stefano opened her door and shielded her from the waiting throng. 'For the moment, of necessity and to save face for my family, we are engaged. Perhaps some of the damage can be repaired. The engagement can be terminated when enough time has passed.'

His statement hit her like a blow to the chest. This day just kept getting worse.

'I'm not pretending any such thing.'

She would not be the outsider again, like during her whole childhood. She wanted to fit. To be loved, not tolerated. To be the centre of someone's universe, not a distant moon floating in his orbit until he was ready to evict her from his gravitational pull.

'It is not pretence.' He pulled a box from his pocket and lifted her unresisting hand, slid on the heavy stone. The ring hung like a shackle from her finger, a monstrous square-cut diamond, mocking her newly engaged status. 'It is temporary.'

'That's all right, then.' A semi-hysterical laugh slipped out. 'I'm used to temporary.'

His hand tightened on hers. 'Can you not see you have done enough damage?'

She felt so tired. What about the damage to *her*?

This time when he took her hand no sparks flew. Their misery separated them completely and she should be grateful for that. What did she expect? That he would take her in his arms and weep with her, say he was sorry he hadn't been there for her? Unlikely. But it would have been nice.

He turned inscrutably to introduce her to those who waited.

She didn't understand any of this. How could a fake engagement help this situation? It would have to end some time. But she tried to smile as she mumbled, 'Hello.' Then she was towed across the forecourt to a line of servants, where another flurry of introductions was performed until finally it was over.

The wall between them must be visible to all who watched, but no doubt the loyalty of his people would colour it differently.

Once inside the palace Stefano dropped her hand and strode ahead, so she followed him up the inner staircase to the family apartments, more unhappy with every step.

They even passed the stained glass doors without opening them—so much for her favourite place—and climbed another staircase to a redwood landing.

He gestured her through some white doors and followed her in. 'These were my mother's rooms. It will be expected that you stay here. There is a turret if you wish for a quiet place to sit until I return. A place to gather your thoughts.'

He was just going to leave her here? Alone?

His face softened a fraction and she thought he was going to say something less harsh, but in the end he shook his head. 'This whole thing is a fiasco. I must see my father.'

And then he was gone.

CHAPTER TEN

MORE OF A tragedy than a fiasco.

Kiki stood, shivering, in the vast apartment with several doors that were closed, like strangers shutting her out. She didn't know what to think or do. She hadn't felt this numb and directionless since that night when her baby had left her.

Stefano strode away, but in the back of his mind was the picture of Kiki's white face and how small she'd looked alone in his mother's rooms. But he had to harden his heart to that because his weakness with this woman had caused all this. He must put aside the guilt that whispered to him that in truth he had not tried hard enough to touch base with a woman who had given him everything he had asked for.

And this new pain—this gnawing emptiness he had never experienced before—could it be the loss of something he had not thought would affect him so powerfully? But over it all was the disgust that he had let his family down again. That he could not forgive. He wasn't even sure where to start to repair the damage.

Kiki had fallen asleep on the sofa, and when she woke Stefano was back, sitting opposite, watching her with an unreadable expression on his aristocratic face.

She sat up, ran her hand through her hair and tried to straighten her clothes unobtrusively. Hard to gather her composure when he continued to stare.

'Do you feel better?' Not friendly, but at least the freezing tone of his voice had risen a few degrees.

She blinked and sat up straighter. 'That depends. Was it all a bad dream?'

He shook his head. 'It is still a bad dream.'

She sighed. 'Then I don't feel better.'

He almost smiled. 'So, I must apologise for assuming you told the papers.'

That was one bright moment in a bad day. 'You believe me?'

He had the grace to look away. 'I have the truth from your doctor friend, Hobson, who has been concerned for your safety.'

She sighed. 'Of course you didn't believe me.' She looked around then, hoping for a glass of water or a cup of tea. Anything for her dry throat. She saw the ring lying on the table where she'd taken it off. 'How long do I have to stay here?'

He too looked at the ring and his eyes narrowed. 'Is the apartment as well as the ring not to your liking?'

She shrugged. 'I haven't seen the rooms. And you haven't answered my question. In fact you've said precious little, and I've had just about enough of being kept in the dark.'

He said implacably, 'You must stay until I say you may go.'

She shook her head and stood up. 'That doesn't work for me.'

It was his turn to sigh. 'Again we are at loggerheads. And if I were to ask what *will* work for you?'

'I need to find a job.' She glared at him. 'Thanks to

you. Find a place to live. Leave this fiasco behind and get on with my life.'

He lifted his hand. Gestured to the room. 'All these things you can do on Aspelicus.'

She shook her head. 'I'm not staying in the palace.'

He shrugged. 'For the moment needs must. But in a few weeks perhaps you could move to the village through the week and stay in the castle during the weekends.'

As she lifted her head to dispute that he went on.

'You will be undisturbed in these apartments, of course, but for the next two weeks at the very least we must be seen together.'

She didn't understand. How could it help her, being here? She didn't want to be reminded every day that he hated her. 'Why perpetuate a myth that will be found out in the end?'

He stood and walked to the window. 'Because my father is old-fashioned. Because he and my people wish desperately for my heir and they are greatly distressed to think I would leave the woman who carried my child alone. The loss of that dream and the blow to my esteem has created a furore. If they think I am engaged to you then not all is lost.'

'Your father hated me from first sight. Let alone now.' The way Prince Paulo had stared her up and down the first time they met had promised little rapport.

'You imagine things. My father is very focussed on the good name of Aspelicus. He believes I should marry a woman of similar social standing, but this is my decision.'

'And mine. And I'm not marrying you.'

'But you will remain engaged to me for the time being, because you owe me that.'

Kiki felt as though her head was going to explode. 'I owe you nothing.'

But he was not having any of it. 'Is two weeks too much to ask? For the damage that has been done?'

She could feel the trap closing. 'Can't we just be seen together at the hospital? I can work with that.'

'In due course.' He stood up. 'For now, there will be a formal reception this evening. You are guest of honour. At seven I will come for you. The timing is poor, with the Prince's Cup next week and all the functions that require my presence.' He looked at her with a cynical smile. 'And now *your* presence too.'

She was sick of it all but too exhausted to fight. What did it matter? She looked down at her crumpled clothes. 'I'm going to look fabulous for the event.'

He stood. 'One of our local designers will take care of everything. She has several outfits she wishes to show you. Please try for a demure neckline.'

Her eyes glittered. 'Shame it isn't fancy dress. She might have a habit and I could go as a nun.'

'You look good in black.' His tone was less than flattering.

'With a wimple? So would you.'

He turned and left and Kiki stared at the closed door. What was she going to do? She had no idea how to survive what he was asking. Especially the way she felt at this moment.

And the wall around him was so thick she couldn't see the man she had once thought she loved. How had this happened? She was alone, held on an island where the ruling family decided whether she could go or stay.

No allies except her family, and she didn't want to involve them until she could see her way out.

Before she could think of anything else there was a knock on the door and a maid brought in some tea and a cake.

Kiki decided the world might look less disastrous if she at least drank something.

By the time she'd finished her tea the designer had arrived and they discussed Kiki's fashion needs for the next two weeks.

It seemed there were mammoth requirements for the Prince's Cup. Shoes and handbags had been chosen, undergarments arrayed.

Of course Stefano hadn't mentioned the beauty technician who arrived to manicure, pedicure and mini-facial her before the hairstylist arrived…

It was perhaps fortunate that Kiki felt like a rag doll, able to be pulled this way and that, because her brain was whirring like a machine as she realised that she was truly officially engaged to a prince—albeit short-term—even if the world thought she had trapped him into it. And she would be expected to know what to do.

For the moment, she let them have their way. Perhaps externally she would look the part, and it required no mental energy from her.

To her surprise, all the attendants seemed genuinely glad to be of service to her, and she wondered why Stefano's subjects didn't hate her for putting him through the gossip mill.

But it seemed that despite what he had said to Kiki personally Stefano had cast her as the victim, not the offender. Shame he didn't believe it himself, because that shift would make this whole scenario so much easier to bear.

She didn't know if she could do this without his support. Her emotions were shot, and she had been getting more fragile every day—until here she was, on the eve of the day she had dreaded for months.

Never would she have believed it would be over-shadowed by something else.

Even some direction on what she should do or say would be helpful in her current fragile state. How dared he not see how lost she was and how in need of support from him, no matter how pressing the affairs of state?

The only other person who might possibly be able to help her was Elise, but the housekeeper had been conspicuous by her absence and, given her extreme loyalty to Stefano, that was not surprising.

Just disappointing, because Elise was the one woman in the palace who would know what was going on. And maybe even understand how Kiki couldn't possibly be responsible for airing something so privately tragic. Elise might just understand because she too had lost her dreams of children.

At one o'clock the attendants had gone. A maid knocked and delivered a small salad and a roll for lunch, and a pot of coffee. Desperately Kiki stopped her as she was about to disappear.

'The housekeeper—Elise. Is she here today?'

'Of course, Dr Fender. Mrs Prost lives in the palace and is on duty whenever Prince Stefano is at home.'

She should have known. No surprises there. *That's how he'd like me,* Kiki thought cynically, *on duty whenever he wants.*

She nodded. 'Lovely. Then could you ask if she has a moment? I would like to see her, please.'

'Of course, Doctor.' The maid curtsied and slipped out through the door.

When Elise arrived, not many minutes later, Kiki wasn't even sure what she was going to say to the housekeeper. One glance at her impassive face showed Elise was withholding her own opinion.

Kiki needed this woman as her ally—she had to have at least one in the castle—and nothing but the truth was going to secure that.

'Please sit down, Elise.'

The woman perched uneasily on the edge of a chair. 'I hope everything is to your satisfaction, Dr Fender?'

The lines were drawn, then. 'I thought we were on a first-name basis?'

'That was before you became engaged to Prince Stefano. It would not be proper now.'

Kiki sighed. 'Fine. I need you to understand that I would never ask you to do anything that would harm Prince Stefano or the royal house of Mykonides.'

The woman's eyes flashed. 'And I would rather die.'

'I had already guessed that.' Kiki smiled. 'It is good to have that said.' She folded her hands in her lap. 'But I also need you to understand that I had nothing to do with publishing or giving the information that was printed by that newspaper.'

'So His Highness has said.'

She wasn't getting anywhere. The woman still distrusted her, and how could she blame her? 'Elise. I met Prince Stefano and we were very drawn to each other. As a woman who has lost her own children surely you

can see that a mother would not share her grief with
the world as has happened to me?'

Elise stilled, stared at her, and finally nodded.

Kiki felt the first glimpse of hope she'd felt all day
and went on.

'I believe the Prince is a good man and is distressed
by the news. Did you know I tried to contact him? I
had no idea his royal duties were so arduous, or that
his recent accident was the reason he didn't answer
me.' She saw the moment Elise understood and finally sighed with relief. 'There is still a chemistry that
neither of us thinks sensible. Now this has happened,
and for the moment at least I must stay here. Behave
as his betrothed. I don't want to let him down again.
But I need help.'

Was that an imperceptible relaxing of her face? Was
she imagining just a little more warmth in the woman's eyes?

'I see.' Elise looked away to the tall windows for
a moment and then looked back. 'And I am sorry for
your loss.' She nodded. 'Yes. You will need help. I
will help.' She added primly, 'Also, I can say there has
been a retraction in the paper, stating the fact that His
Highness was gravely injured at the time of your miscarriage, and that he found you only a few days ago.
Things do not look so bad when the true facts come to
light. Legal action has commenced.'

Kiki could almost spare a thought for Ginger and
her boyfriend. Almost.

Elise stood up. 'I can see that it will help if you sail
smoothly through the next two weeks.' She paused at
the door. 'I will return with your itinerary and discuss what is required of you.'

* * *

For Kiki, at least, things improved after that. Elise's support, once offered, was beyond generous. By the time Stefano came to escort his new fiancée to dinner she knew the correct curtsies, the names of the five most important people she would meet, and the itinerary for the evening. Even the menu.

It felt good to have a little more control.

And Elise's final suggestion had come in words from her late princess—'God rest her soul.'

She'd told her, 'See only one person or the occasion will overwhelm you. Look, speak and smile at one person and you will be in control of the room.'

Kiki nodded. Sound advice and she'd certainly try. Because it seemed that no help would come from the man who had let her down when she most needed him. *Again.*

Kiki wore a classic black floor-length gown, with just enough cleavage to say, *so this is why the man is smitten.* Her dark hair had been artfully piled on top of her head, and with her faultless make-up her composure appeared complete. Too complete. Because she felt like a figurine in a wax museum—incredibly lifelike but numb to sensation. But she would get through this without his help.

Stefano didn't know what to expect when he reached the door to his mother's rooms. He hoped Kiki was still not slouched in the chair.

When he opened the door, for the first time in his life Prince Stefano Mykonides felt intimidated.

She looked at him with such indifference his blood chilled.

'I am ready, Your Highness.'

His Dr Fender looked like a film star.

The besieged and crushed victim whom he'd res-cued from the press had been replaced by a self-as-sured young woman waiting calmly and coldly to take his arm.

He glanced around the apartment as if to see the other person he'd expected. This woman did not look out of place. The room could have been designed for she who consistently stunned him when he least ex-pected it.

The grandmother clock in the corner chimed and he was jolted back into reality. Now was not the time to mull over questions that required thoughtful answers.

'Of course. Let us go.'

She put her hand on his arm without hesitation as he led the way and her fingers did not waver. It was his turn to feel the wall between them.

All rose as they entered. Kiki smiled slightly and nodded—not effusively, but that was good. She curt-sied to his father with such gracefulness that even the women of the court smiled and Stefano felt his chest swell just a little with pride. This morning he would never have dreamed that she would carry this off so magnificently. This morning there had been no pride to be had.

'She has presence,' his father grunted for his ears alone. 'But it remains to be seen if you have ruined someone else's life by your reckless actions.'

Stefano felt familiar guilt chill the pleasure he had gained in the moment and he glanced at Kiki. Some-thing in her expression made him wonder if she'd over-heard. He could only hope not.

When he seated her beside him she answered his questions, but there was still the distance that had been there since he'd collected her. A gulf so wide he could see no way of bridging it. He assured himself that was good.

She seemed to prefer to converse quietly with the Mayor, on her right at the table, and yet he, the more practised statesman, was too much aware of her. Probably just the upheavals of the day.

The evening continued to unnerve him. He had been prepared to protect her, gloss over the mistakes she wouldn't see, but she required no help.

Kiki nodded and smiled and held her composure with concentration. If she excluded the grandeur of the surroundings and the glitter of the people and concentrated on one person at a time she found her advice held good.

Especially if she blocked Stefano out.

Just in that first moment before they'd left, when he'd entered her rooms to escort her, he'd looked so tall and forbidding in black tails and the royal sash, with jewelled medals flashing, she'd mentally faltered.

But only for a moment, before she'd stoked up her anger. She'd concentrated on the person, searched behind the regalia and remembered the man who had left her without support and now expected her to fail in such unfamiliar and challenging surroundings.

That had been inexcusable, and the reminder had protected her from any connection that would discomfort her—until she'd heard that muttered judgement from Prince Paulo.

It had been a glimpse into Stefano's life and what he dealt with every day. She remembered his comment that his mother had been the lighter-natured of the two. She could see that now, and despite herself felt herself soften and sympathise with Stefano.

She glanced across to the old Prince and unexpectedly caught his eye. She glared at him, glad the engagement was a farce, because she didn't need a person like that permanently in her life. He blinked. Grumpy old man. She turned away.

If tonight's disapproval had been there all Stefano's life no wonder he could become tense with pressure.

She could sense him beside her now. Feel the awareness that seemed to inhabit the space between them even when they were not conversing. But she couldn't afford to lay her hand on his arm and express the sympathy she wanted to because she needed to stay focussed until she could return to the safety of her room. But perhaps she understood him a little more.

Luckily the gentleman beside her could converse easily, with little prompting from her. The Mayor of Aspelicus was one of the five Elise had mentioned, so she knew his role in the business, and that his son was in charge of festivities for the Prince's Cup. He did seem delighted with her knowledge and her appreciation of his heavy civil duties, and mentally she thanked Elise for her tutelage.

Eventually the older gentleman excused himself to answer a question from another table companion and Kiki had to turn back to Stefano.

He raised his brows. 'And how is my old friend Bruno Valinari?'

Kiki smiled, because in a lesser man he would have sounded almost petulant. 'He is well. And proud of his son—as he should be. And how is your dinner and your evening, Your Highness?'

His mouth came down level with her cheek and she tried not to inhale the subtle tang of his aftershave, because it floated too many memories for a state function. Tried not to look at the strong cheekbones and carved mouth as he drew closer.

'I am wondering if there is to be any attention from my fiancée.'

Subtly she drew back further. 'You'll survive without my attention.' She raised her brows. 'As I did without yours today.' She met his eyes. 'Did it occur to you I could have done with a little guidance from you?'

'My apologies. My duties constrained me.' His glance travelled over her. 'Though I see no lack in your instruction.'

'Gee, thanks.' She could play that game. 'How unusual for you *not* to see something.'

His eyes gleamed. 'So the cat has claws.'

Kiki sat straighter in her chair and even leaned a little to the right to increase the distance between them. She kept the smile on her face but there was none in her voice. 'I'm not duelling with you at this table.'

Actually, when it came down to it, she couldn't. She didn't have the headspace.

She glanced around for a friendly face and Marla waved her fingers discreetly from across the table. Kiki realised she did have another ally in the palace. When people began to circulate, perhaps she could excuse herself and cross over to Marla. The chance to seek out her supposed future sister-in-law would help enormously.

She changed the subject. 'I see Theros and Marla are here. They look happy.'

Stefano turned to look at his brother and his face became more guarded. 'Yes. It is good to see him not as restless as usual.'

That seemed a strange thing to say. 'So he is normally restless?'

He glanced around to see if anyone had overheard. 'That also is not for this table.'

No-go zones made life even more difficult, but what did she expect when in truth she knew little about his family? 'In that case it's your turn to start a conversation or I'll go back to Bruno.'

He smiled and inclined his head, and the appreciation in his eyes made the heat rise in her own face. She jammed the rising weakness back into its box.

'You look beautiful. And confident. I applaud you.'

Maybe he should go back to mocking her, because compliments played havoc with that very composure. 'Thank you.' She glanced at his father, who watched them both from under fierce white brows, and then back at Stefano. 'It could just be confidence from designer clothes and my own stylist.'

'Perhaps. Perhaps not. We shall see. Tomorrow you must meet the people. Two more critical children have flown in for surgery and I must go to the hospital. As soon as they are stabilised I will be in surgery.'

She wanted to ask more but he went on.

'Unfortunately the new wing—funded by last year's Prince's Cup—is to be opened. Now I cannot be there and my father's advisors have requested you attend with him.' He mocked her. 'Are you free?'

As if she had so much to do. And what if she said no? But just the idea of getting away from the palace made her feel better. She thought of the hospital and her spirits lifted. 'Of course. And could I visit the children as well?'

His eyes shuttered. 'I doubt there will be time.' He shrugged. 'You will be busy with your duties. It is only to be a short visit.'

The flattening of her spirits at his refusal did more to unnerve her than anything the glittering room could achieve. That he could so nonchalantly ignore the fact that to visit the children would give her pleasure seemed so out of character for the man she'd thought he was. It hurt anew.

Someone spoke to him from his left and she sank back in the seat. Sank back, not relaxed back, because foolishly she looked along the row of guests, most of whom glanced her way every few seconds, and knew this wasn't her natural habitat. She'd never get used to it—didn't want to get used to it, because in fact she disliked the grandeur, the formality, the opulence of it all intensely. At this moment she also disliked Stefano intensely, and this was where Stefano belonged. Not her.

When she glanced down to the end of the table a man smiled at her and she realised it was Dr Franco Tollini from the other day. She raised her brows and smiled and let her gaze drift away. Complications were too hard. Her head was above water—just—and she wanted to keep it that way.

She lifted her spoon and tasted the dessert but she didn't want it. Too much food.

How did Stefano keep so fit? He was all lean muscle and power...and perhaps she shouldn't let her thoughts drift there while she was being watched by a hundred eyes. Thankfully, Bruno turned to her and asked a question before she lost herself in remembering just how weak she was when he held her in his arms and how she had arrived at this moment.

Finally the long dinner was over. Nobody circulated, and Kiki had never felt more trapped. They bade good-night to the Crown Prince, who glanced over them both coldly, and then to Kiki's relief they bumped into Marla and Theros. Stefano seemed reluctant to chat, but Kiki made a point of asking Marla how she was.

Before she could answer her husband chimed in with, 'Catwoman. Meow.'

Theros grinned at her and Kiki blushed. Stefano stepped in and took his brother's arm, steered him away. Kiki wasn't sure what had happened.

She looked at Marla, who smiled apologetically. 'I'm well.' She glanced at her husband and lowered her voice. 'He's an absolute darling but he has no social skills.'

It seemed a strange thing to say about a prince, but Marla went on warmly.

'What about you? I thought you were so brave, coming tonight.'

That made her laugh for the first time of the night. 'I didn't have much choice.'

Before she could enlarge on that Stefano returned with a subdued Theros, and Marla whispered, 'Let's catch up tomorrow,' before she caught her husband's hand and led him away.

Something wasn't right, and Kiki frowned after them, but all she could think was that perhaps the younger prince had had too much to drink.

CHAPTER ELEVEN

STEFANO STEERED HER in the other direction. 'Come. It is late and we both have a big day tomorrow.'

His hand was on her arm again, and she didn't know how much more of this hot and cold treatment she could take. Her physical awareness of him beside her only made her more cross. Judging by the way his hand came over hers on his arm, he might have picked up on the vibe that she was about to shake him off.

Stefano meant to leave her at the door and stride away. Because if he didn't there was a risk he would sweep her into his arms and forget everything. But he wasn't that man.

That man who had temporarily ignored the responsibilities of his station.

That one lapse.

Once in his life he had allowed his heart to rule his head and look what had happened. But he could not rid himself of the look of hurt in Kiki's eyes and his own heart ached in a way he had never felt before.

When he let her go to open the doors to her suite Kiki paused as he looked down at her. She stared at him, as if trying to see beneath his skin, and the moment stilled. The ever-present sounds of the grand-mother clock faded and their eyes met and held.

Here they were, and for the first time that evening Kiki had time to feel like putting her head in her hands to mourn what they had lost.

How had they found themselves at such logger-heads? How had she ended up here, 'temporarily en-gaged' to the man she had tragically made a child with?

What series of events, trends of fate and plain bad luck had mocked them both and put such obstacles in the way of a woman and a man who were attracted?

'What happened to us, Stefano?' Kiki asked care-fully.

Again he let her down. Just compressed his lips and shuttered his eyes.

'Almost everything. We must try to make the best of this disastrous situation while I deal with it.'

Her temper flared. 'I am not a "disastrous situa-tion". I am a respected medical practitioner who has been kidnapped.'

She saw him glance around to check they were alone before he steered her through into the rooms, closed the doors and stood with his back to them. 'Please try and remember what happens when people overhear things they shouldn't.'

She was sick of worrying about what others thought. 'Why do you think you can shut me out? Why do you need to control everything? Do you think it actually changes fate? Life is learning to live with what hap-pens.'

One of them needed to be honest.

She gestured to the room. 'Everything is different here. *You're* different. Especially now I've seen a small part of what your lifestyle entails and how it changes you.' She stepped up to him and he watched her with very little expression on his face. She wished he would react at least. 'This control freak is not the man I fell in love with.'

He blinked when she said she'd loved him.

'I need control.'

The words seemed almost torn from him and she stopped, arrested by the expression on his face.

Some nuance captured her attention, cut through her distress, sharpened her instincts. 'Why do you need control?'

He stepped away from the door, walked past her towards the settee she'd slept on earlier.

'How do you find my brother?'

She frowned. That was random. She almost said, *I'd look for Marla*, but she didn't want to talk about Theros. 'He seems nice.' She thought for a moment, and then a suspicion began to form in her mind. Something Marla had said. And Stefano had said Theros was restless. 'Is there something wrong with Theros?'

He sighed. 'You know Mikey's brother—Chris—he woke up. He'll be fine.'

Another random comment. Or was it?

'I'm glad.' She sat down beside him as he stared straight ahead. She waited.

Finally he began to speak. 'There was an accident when we were children. Theros almost drowned in an ocean pool. I managed to resuscitate him but not fast enough. He is a child in a man's body because of me.'

She lowered her voice. It all began to make sense. Guilt. Shame. Loss of control. 'How old were you?'

'Eight.' Still he stared straight ahead, and somehow

she knew he had never spoken about this to anyone. She couldn't understand how he had kept it from being common knowledge.

'Eight years old?' Her stomach dropped and she wanted to take his head in her hands and kiss him for the years of pain and self-flagellation she could now see he had been determined to endure. Had probably been *encouraged* to endure, if she'd read his father right. But she needed to speak carefully if he was ever to have peace. 'And you resuscitated your drowned brother?'

He flexed his shoulders. 'Not quickly enough to prevent damage.'

She said, 'You resuscitated your drowned brother, by yourself, so that he breathed again?'

'Yes.'

She saw him blink. Consider. Finally use his powerful brain to think about himself. He closed his eyes.

She persisted. 'Would you have blamed Mikey if he had done the same?'

His eyes flew open and he sat straighter. 'Of course not.'

She stared at him, but he refused to meet her determined gaze with his own. She lowered her voice but knew he heard every word. 'Then perhaps it is time to forgive yourself.'

Finally he looked at her. 'I fear I am destined to hurt the ones I love.'

She nodded and took his hand, stroked the strong fingers that had held her through memorable nights, felt his pain and rested his fingers against her heart. She understood him so much more.

'And that is the dilemma. Perhaps it's time to let go that which can't be changed. Perhaps consider that happiness doesn't need perfection. Theros seems very happy.'

Stefano looked down at the slender fingers that stroked his and felt the weight of the years grow imperceptibly lighter. Just a little. He thought about his brother. Smiled at the thought. 'He *is* happy when he isn't in trouble with me.' He could acknowledge that if he allowed himself to consider it.

She put his hand back down and moved hers away. 'Then let it go. You can't control everything.'

How did she do that? Suggest gently and steer him towards peace when he'd carried guilt like a blanket made of lead around his shoulders for as long as he could remember?

The grandmother clock began to chime and neither of them spoke as the toll rang out until midnight was proclaimed.

Suddenly Kiki realised the day she had dreaded was here. But, despite his presence, Stefano wasn't with her for that.

She stood up. God, she was so tired. And there was so much to think about. Tonight she was going to try and do the same thing she'd told Stefano to do, because she'd promised herself that when this day came she would let go.

'Please leave. I'm tired and I can't think any more.'

She knew he could sense her withdrawal, so she was surprised when he asked, 'What if I don't want to go?'

She turned her back on him, because she didn't have the reserves to fight. 'I can't help that,' she said. And she walked away.

After an emotional discussion with her pillow Kiki slept fitfully. She was woken by Elise with coffee and croissants and a warning that soon the stylist would arrive to prepare her for a day of official functions.

Every time her mind wandered to the significance of the date she pushed it away.

The really bad news came with her breakfast. She must travel with Crown Prince Paulo in the official convoy.

She sipped her tea pensively. What the heck could she talk about? Or maybe you didn't talk to the Crown Prince—though an hour of disapproving silence would be like water torture.

By the time she was handed into the official car she was feeling more sure than ever that she wasn't cut out for this life. And the royal scrutiny was such that she couldn't tell if he was satisfied with her appearance or not.

'Good morning, Dr Fender.'

'Good morning, Prince Paulo.' She slid into the car past the footman holding the door.

'Did you sleep well?'

Apparently he did talk, and Kiki felt herself relax slightly. She usually did after a big cry. 'It was a different sleep than on the ship.'

'Of course.'

He transferred his attention to the cobbled streets of the castle forecourt as they began their journey and Kiki sighed. That was that, then.

How had she ended up in a royal car with an autocratic old despot?

'If you don't mind me asking, why am I with you today, Prince Paulo?'

The Prince turned back to her. 'Because Stefano is not. Too often he neglects his royal duties for his passion with surgery.' He glanced back out of the window. 'And see where that gets him.'

Kiki's sense of fairness disputed that. Couldn't he see the good Stefano did? The depth of care and kindness his son showed his patients was admirable, even if that kindness didn't extend to *her* at the present time.

Kiki narrowed her eyes on the back of the Prince's head. 'Your son saves lives. Has there not been a physician in your family since the first Mykonides?'

That turned his head. Now he was every inch the monarch. His bristled white brows soared, his eyes narrowed, and in that moment she saw the dark eyes of his son at their most arctic.

'Who are you to presume to tell me my own history?'

But strangely Kiki wasn't afraid or uncomfortable. It was as if a calm voice whispered in her ear to let him bluster.

She should say *she* was the woman pretending to be engaged to his son to help the family's good name. But she didn't need this man as her enemy.

'My apologies, Your Highness.'

But they both knew she wasn't cowed by him, and she wondered if she could detect just a glimpse of approval in his eyes.

In a more conciliatory tone she went on, 'I'm saying his skills as a surgeon are a gift.'

The Prince shrugged and allowed himself to stop pretending he was enraged. 'So they say.' He turned to look out of the window and she heard him mutter, 'He should be more of a prince.'

Kiki turned to her own window as they began their

spiral descent of the mountain. 'He could hardly be more.'

She heard the indrawn breath of the old man but she couldn't regret it. What could he do? Put her out of the car. Well, she was happy with that idea.

'So you champion a man who leaves you pregnant in another country?'

It seemed the old man had rallied.

They faced each other like circling dogs.

'Circumstances were not kind to us.'

'If he has any of me in him he will not be kind to you either.' He glared at her, and then slowly his gaze softened. 'You remind me of someone I knew long ago. She too was fearless.' He laughed without amusement. 'And stubborn. This may not turn out badly yet.'

Kiki had nothing to say to that. Now she felt less sure of herself, and wondered what had possessed her to take him on.

The drive through the olive groves passed silently and Kiki chewed on her lip as she worried what would be asked of her today.

Finally the Prince roused himself. 'I think you should address the women. The patronesses. It is a gynaecological ward we are opening. Thank them for their donations which have helped create the facility and they will be happy.'

Her worst nightmare. What should she say? 'Surely they would prefer your address to mine?'

'Ha! You are a woman.' He turned away. 'I have decided.'

Typical. Like father, like son, she thought with an unhappy sigh.

* * *

As Kiki came to the end of her speech—more of a lecture on meeting health needs as all women deserved—than an informal thank-you, and Prince Paulo seemed happy enough. It had proved less of a trial than she had anticipated. But it had been stressful, and underneath she seethed.

She'd had an epiphany. Here she was for these women, and today of all days Stefano, of course, was not here for *her*.

Kiki estimated there were about fifty well-dressed women, most of them around her age. With women's health so important she'd spoken from the heart, because that way at least she could be happy with what she said.

Until she asked for questions and of course the most difficult one surfaced.

Kiki looked at the woman and something warned her. Despite her designer clothes, her coiffed hair, she had sad, sad eyes, and Kiki knew this woman struggled in a dark place too.

The woman moistened her lips and Kiki leaned forward slightly to hear. 'Are you afraid of miscarrying again?'

Kiki sighed and nodded. 'But as a doctor I remind myself that one miscarriage, or even two miscarriages, does not mean I am more at risk. Yes, it crosses my mind, but I have to trust in the future.'

The woman smiled gently, closed her eyes and nodded. Then she whispered, 'I lost my baby last month.'

Kiki felt her eyes sting and stepped down off the little podium. The others parted to let her through, and the two women embraced. Quietly, but unashamedly, so it carried to everyone in the room, Kiki said, 'My baby would have been due today.'

When they drew apart and smiled mistily at each other Kiki knew she had found a friend, and for the first time she thought perhaps there *were* things she could achieve here if she and Stefano ever worked it out. But at this moment that seemed very unlikely. And the waste made her angrier.

Out of the corner of her eye she saw Prince Paulo gesture to the Mayor to conclude the event, and she mentally prepared herself for the trip back with the Prince.

Bruno directed her to the podium again and then turned to the audience. 'Thank you so much, Dr Fender, for your sincerity. We are all deeply appreciative of your presence today.'

Kiki stepped back, the crowd began to disperse, and she gathered her emotions and control. Just.

Until she saw Stefano arrive and cross to his father. She narrowed her eyes. Typical. *Great timing,* she thought, *when it's too late to support me, but in time to judge me.* Her anger stepped up another notch. Of all days she had had to do this and he didn't even know.

Stefano spoke briefly to his father and she saw Prince Paulo pat his son's shoulder in an unusual gesture of affection. He nodded in her direction, and with his entourage cordially turned away.

Stefano crossed to her side. He seemed bemused. 'My father said you did well. That the women liked you. Congratulations.'

Something snapped inside her. 'Gee, thanks.' She saw he didn't miss the sarcasm and was glad. How dared he? She 'did well'? So magnanimous of him.

Was she supposed to be thrilled at his approval? And what if she hadn't done well? Would he have been here to support her?

His gaze narrowed. 'You're angry? With me?'

'Do you know what I told them?'

He shook his head warily, and she could feel emotion bubbling when she wanted to be ice-cold. Angry tears stung her eyes and she turned away from him, because the words wouldn't come. She wanted them to spill out, hurt him as they hurt her, but she couldn't make her mouth work.

He followed her as she walked blindly along the corridor back towards the entrance, and once he steered her gently when she would have taken a wrong turn.

Stefano didn't know what to do. He could see that Kiki seethed with emotion. Had he pushed her too far by expecting her to do this today? But he'd had to operate. He reminded himself that she hadn't been trained for these occasions as he had, and yet every time he asked something of her she responded magnificently. But at what cost?

She swept out of the hospital and he kept pace, nodding at those he passed as if it was his decision to continue this headlong race she had begun. She stopped at his car and spun to face him. The look in her eyes made him step back.

'Do you know what you asked of me today?'

He didn't want to know right here, right now, because it was not going to be pretty. He opened her door. 'Please, first sit.'

She opened and shut her mouth, and with relief he saw she would do as he asked. When he slid behind the wheel her emotion was like a wall between them and he put up his hand as if to touch it.

'Can I ask you to wait a few more minutes? For the privacy you deserve, not for me. I wish to give you my undivided attention.'

Again she nodded, and he started the car and drove along the road until he came to a lay-by that overlooked the olive groves. He turned the engine off and faced her.

Finally the words spilled like bullets, and he winced.

'Since yesterday morning my life has not been my own.' She drew a breath. 'You have accused me of many things, all of them incorrect, and you have constantly thrown me into situations that were beyond my control.'

He knew it was true. Last night, when he'd finally stopped thinking about himself, he had begun to realise just what he had put her through. And yet still she had been there for him. The more he had considered it the more he'd been able to see how he had failed her.

He deserved every accusation for the mistakes he'd made. For the need he couldn't let go of to maintain control over his life. He wanted to say he was sorry for whatever he'd done, to hold her, comfort her. But the wall between them kept him back.

'Can you tell me what happened in there?'

She jabbed her finger towards his head. 'Can *you* tell me what happens in *there*? In your closely guarded mind that simply refuses to open to me. To trust.' She shook her head with frustration. 'You expect so little from me...'

'No.'

'Yes,' Kiki insisted. 'You would rather think I am a woman who will fail you than a woman who can succeed. I can succeed at anything.' She looked at him sadly. 'And I can succeed without you, Stefano.'

'You have more than proved that.' And then he looked at her. 'Not once have you failed me. It is the other way round.'

'I know. Why is that?'

He had no answer. He watched her shudder against the door as she leaned as far away as possible from him. His hand clenched uselessly, because he couldn't mistake her aversion to any movement towards her on his part.

She stared out through the front windshield. 'Today I was there for those women in a way you have never been for me. And it came home to me just how much you have let me down. The waste when we could have been so good. And, yes, it makes me very angry.'

She pointed an accusing finger at him.

'I gave more than I thought I would have to. Again without your support. In the last few days I have been forced to publicly expose my pain again and again—and you know what? I can't do it any more.'

She was right, and he hastened to reassure her. 'I won't ask it of you.'

She turned towards him and he saw the tears in her eyes, could feel her hurt in his own chest. She finally lifted her chin. As always, her strength astounded him.

He could hear the control she clung to in her voice. 'You've missed the whole point of what I needed from you. Especially today.'

The words captured him. Something in her voice… 'Why today?'

She didn't answer that right away, and he almost missed the significance—again.

'Because it's heartbreaking to lose a baby. And today should have been about life. Not loss.'

, 'Today?' The full import of what she was saying finally seeped into his consciousness along with the anguish in her voice.

He read the confirmation on Kiki's face and realised he truly did deserve to lose not only his child but this woman. And just when he'd come to understand how much he needed her in his life.

That he didn't ever want to lose her.

Couldn't lose her.

He was so afraid he had finally completely driven her away?

Stefano knew it was time to battle his own demons. To risk everything. Because if he didn't he would lose the best thing that had ever happened to him. He reached for her, and to his shuddering relief this time she didn't pull away.

He slid his finger under her chin and gently turned her to him, so he could cradle her face in his hands, stare into her beautiful eyes. 'I am so sorry.'

He saw the reflection of his own sense of loss for what they'd had between them and ached to ease her pain.

'I am sorry,' he said again, and sighed. Why did he always do and say the wrong thing around this woman? 'What I have done to you is unforgivable.' He reflected over the last twenty-four hours and winced. His voice was bitter at his own stupidity. 'My bullying and my anger at the public scrutiny didn't take into account the cost to you.'

Mental screenshots flickered past like a horror film—the way he had dragged her to the palace, thrust his mother's ring on her finger, installed her in his mother's isolated rooms with barely an explanation. Left her alone to suffer while he'd worried more about others.

To make matters a hundred times worse he had then forced her to attend a ceremonial function that very night—most probably because he had truly expected her to fail. Then he would have been able to tell himself it would never work.

How could she ever love the monster he had become?

He heard the rasp as she drew in her breath. Watched her blink away the tears that glittered on her lashes as she raised her head.

He had lost her.

'I was a monster to you.'

'Yes, you were.' But then she hugged him. 'All that and more.' She shifted her head back a little, so she could focus. 'Why?'

He had nothing left to give her but the truth. 'Because I was afraid.'

'Of me?'

'Of course of you.' He ran his hands through his hair. 'Of losing control of my life.'

She shook her head. He could see she didn't understand that he knew she was already gone. That he knew he'd knew left his run too late.

She said again. 'What are you talking about?'

'Already I have hurt you in so many ways because of my fears. I will take you back to the mainland this afternoon.'

'You still don't get it. I don't want to go. You've been horrible, but I'll survive.'

His hand lifted and one finger stroked her silken cheek. 'Of course you will survive. You are magnificent. Last night you rose and faced them all as if you had been born to stand head and shoulders above the world.' He was so proud of her, and ashamed of being the man who had subjected her to that. 'No thanks to me.'

She went on in the same hard little voice. 'And today I was there for those women in a way you have never been for me. It came home to me just how much you have let me down. And, yes, it makes me very angry.'

Her lips tilted, teased him, and his fear eased a little that she could still smile his way.

'Some things I *can* thank you for. You rescued me from the press at the dock.'

'Pah.' He snapped his fingers. 'That is nothing. I should not have left you. Well before that I was not there when you needed me the most.'

Stefano leant across and gathered her in next to him, felt her slight weight against him and wanted to protect her from the world. It had taken him too long to realise that was his mission.

'You are here now,' she said.

He drew her even closer. 'Is it true that our baby was to have been born today?'

She nodded her head against him. Whispered, 'Yes,' and his heart contracted.

He moistened his lips, prayed she would hear the truth in his words, and finally said what he should have said when he'd first found out that they had made a baby together. 'I am so sorry I was not there with you when our child slipped away from us.'

Her eyes shadowed as she returned to her most painful memory, allowed him to see through a small window to how it had been. She acknowledged his right to see, and he realised that was the greatest gift she had given him yet.

'It was night and I was alone.' Kiki pressed her lips together to stop their wobble.

He closed his eyes and breathed deeply, more ashamed than he had ever been in all his life. 'My poor, poor love. I wish I could have held you and shared your grief. I should have been there. Let me share it now.' He squeezed her to him as he felt the dampness of his own eyes. 'Please.'

Kiki turned her face into his chest and he stroked her hair as she remembered that night in the hospital. Her tiny, solitary room, dark and metallic, the loneliest place in the world when the pains had increased. Within minutes the bleeding had been so great that by the time a nurse arrived and rushed her off to Theatre her life had almost drained away.

She whispered into the silence between them, in a tiny sports car pulled over at the side of the road, on an island in the Mediterranean Sea with her prince beside her.

'I knew that when I woke up from the anaesthetic it would be gone. Not just our baby, but any link to you.'

And then the tears came, great gulping sobs, and the tearing of her heart that she could finally share with Stefano as she was wrapped in the very arms she'd needed so badly that night so many lonely nights ago. And at last, after far too long, the final healing could begin.

Stefano held her tightly against him, gathering her shudders of grief as he gathered her closer, inhaling the scent of her hair, stroking her over and over again with all the tenderness he had in him. He had never felt as close to anyone in his whole life as he did to this woman at this moment. Had never allowed himself to do so in case he lost himself. But now he wanted to be lost.

Lost with her.

Random flashes of his past with Kiki rolled through his mind.

The first time he'd seen her, like a ray of sunshine in his day, radiant, confident, joyous. A heroine on her quest to help mankind.

The first time he'd held her hand and sensed there was something between them that defied description yet was instantly recognisable—something he would never forget despite all the obstacles fate had thrown up against them.

And that magical week when she had opened her home, her arms and her heart just for him. Stefano the man—not Stefano the Prince. Even when he'd been away, recovering, she'd been like a shadow behind him that refused to be forgotten.

He would make it up to her. He would make it all up to her. He just hoped she felt the same about him, because now that he had her back in his arms he didn't think he could let her go. Ever.

Slowly her weeping turned to hiccups and her flood of tears to a trickle. He mopped her face and hugged her again and kissed her damp mouth gently. He wanted to repeat his apology, but he was afraid she would weep all over again.

But Kiki was made of sterner stuff than that. One last sniff, the hijacking of his handkerchief, and she wiped her eyes and blew her nose resolutely. 'I'm sorry.

That was torrential. Thank you for letting me soak your shirt.'

The knot in his stomach loosened. 'You are very welcome.'

She sniffed again and smiled, with a tiny wobble still in evidence. 'Thank you, anyway. I think I needed that.'

He watched the old Kiki emerge and sat back on his side of the car with bemusement and wonder. Relief expanded in his chest as he realised she had already begun to forgive him. Now all he had to do was forgive himself.

Kiki screwed up the handkerchief after one last trumpeting blow. If he still fancied her after this then there was hope for them yet. But that thought and all it involved was terrifying.

'Thank you for listening, and for being here now.' She glanced around at the grove of olives across the road. 'But perhaps we should talk of something else.'

He didn't move.

'Or head back to the castle?'

The way his gaze moved across her face made her cheeks burn. His grey eyes were softer than she'd ever seen them, and he kissed her fingers and brushed her cheek with a gesture. More heat to her red face, and she looked away, embarrassed, suddenly remembering again that this man was a prince and she'd sobbed all over him.

'How was I so fortunate as to find you?' He shook his head in wonder, and as if unable to help himself reached and took her hand.

They both gazed down at the ring he'd insisted she wear. The huge square diamond flashed with reflected light even when there didn't seem to be any beams to catch. It wasn't hers. Not really.

He leaned forward and spoke very slowly and gently. 'So, my question is this. To the world we are already engaged. But the man who demanded this did not deserve you.'

He stroked the ring on her finger and drew it off. To her dismay, she felt bereft. So this was where they faced the truth. She drew in a breath and steadied herself for the end.

He raised her hand to his lips and caressed her knuckles with his mouth. 'May I start again?'

She blinked, not sure what he meant. A crazy, stuttering hope like a flame caught in a cross breeze tossed her into confusion. Start again? With what?

Stefano searched her face, saw her turmoil, and knew it was time to be brave as this woman had been brave. To lose himself for ever and hand her the power to destroy his world if she willed it. He'd never thought he would see this moment.

He drew a deeper breath. 'Do you know that I love you?'

Her eyes flared and she opened her beautiful mouth and closed it. Then finally she said, 'No.'

His tension increased as she shook her head. How to convince her? 'I love you and wish to spend my life with you. To respect and honour you. But only if this is what you want too.'

He saw the fear, understood she had glimpsed what that would mean and seen not all of it was good. None knew more than he that he asked for an enormous commitment. 'Will you share my life with me as my princess. Do me the honour of being my wife? Wear this ring always?'

She looked down at the ring in his hand. Remembered the weight of it. Could she? Rules and etiquette... Royal crises and functions... Their work at the hospital would keep them busy enough. She thought of the women, of the first of many friends she could make, of those she could help.

Then Kiki imagined a life never seeing Stefano again, losing her dream of dark-haired arrogant little boys like Stefano and tiny little girls in pink tulle, and there was no contest. She would not be alone. She would have Stefano the person. Not the heir to the throne. Just her gorgeous man. Stefano.

She leaned across and kissed him softly on the lips. 'I love you. Will always love you. And that's enough for me.'

He slid the ring back on her finger with immense satisfaction. 'Then that is a yes.'

CHAPTER TWELVE

KIKI'S BROTHER NICK and her sister-in-law had arrived to save her. Instead they accepted an invitation to the Prince's Cup.

This year, when the glitterati arrived on the Friday night before the race, a huge stage had been set in the centre of the racetrack with the sea as its background and festooned with a thousand lights.

There was to be a magnificent celebration for the engagement of Prince Stefano Mykonides and his bride-to-be Dr Kristina Karine Fender and the whole island was invited.

Open-sided marquees were provided for the guests to wander through, eat and drink, barbecue steaks, and strange Australian damper, while they listened to music from among the world's greatest musicians—including Kiki's favourite Australian band, flown over at the last minute.

As a gift and gesture of acknowledgment Stefano had set up a huge screen—a never-ending light show depicting the glory of his betrothed's homeland. From harbour to Outback, it showed soaring scenery, a bird's-eye view circumnavigating the whole coastline and across the continent. From Barrier Reef, to Uluru, the screen breathed life into a continent thousands of miles away, so that his people understood that he was a part of that world as his bride was now a part of theirs.

And through it all Kiki and Stefano walked among the people, shaking hands, smiling at each other and at the world. For Kiki, the magnitude of the spectacle had started as a challenge—but then she'd met people she knew: Dr Herore and her husband. Rosa's family plus Sheba and the new baby. Elise had brought her son, and to Kiki's surprise, Jerome. Stefano had whispered that Elise had asked for his thoughts on adoption.

She began to enjoy meeting the hundreds of people they spoke to, all eager to wish them well and ask about the wedding.

Kiki's brother Nick and his very pregnant wife, Tara, shook their heads repeatedly at his little sister's surprise rise to fame.

Wilhelm and Miko from the ship were there, and audaciously, Miko kissed Kiki's hand right in front of her fiancée. Kiki laughed and Stefano growled good-naturedly about it being his last chance to do so.

But finally, well after midnight, it was over, and Stefano kissed her as soon as they were through the door of their apartments.

'I have been waiting to do this all night.'

It felt so good to have his arms around her and feel the world just disappear.

She sighed happily as she lay back in his arms. 'When I marry you will the wedding be big?'

He laughed ruefully. 'Bigger than you can imagine. It will be a marathon. But at the end we will have each other.'

She leaned across and kissed him softly on the lips. 'Then that's enough for me.'

EPILOGUE

SIX MONTHS LATER, in the red silk-lined formal throne room of the palace, arranged in front of the huge gold fireplace and the soaring portraits of the current ruler and his late princess, in the presence of Prince Paulo, Prince Theros and his wife Princess Marla, a dozen dignitaries, and the bride's four siblings and their partners, a civil ceremony of marriage was carried out by His Excellency the Mayor, Bruno Valinari.

Kiki, dressed in coral-coloured Dior, sat straight-backed, her hands folded demurely in her lap, as she listened to the long legal discourse required before Stefano could legally make her his princess.

Finally the moment came, and without hesitation his voice decreed his intention. 'I pledge my life and legally bind myself to Kristina Karine Fender. My Princess.' And then softly, with joy and belief as he met her eyes, 'My Kiki.'

The Mayor said, 'For ever?'

'I do.'

Her eyes stung, but she knew she couldn't cry. She wondered if princesses were allowed to cry. She'd meant to ask Elise.

Then it was her turn, and she listened, minute after

minute, to the legal jargon mixed with advice in the way of royal wedding ceremonies for the last five hundred years on this sovereign island discovered by pirates and ruled by physicians.

The longer the discourse went on the more nervous she became. Her heart began to pound. She would miss her cue, would stumble, would open her mouth and no sound would come out.

Suddenly she became conscious that tomorrow, in the cathedral, it would be a thousand times worse, with millions upon millions of television viewers. What if her words got stuck?

The Mayor's words seemed to join together in her ears, so she couldn't tell where one began and the other ended, and the lump in her throat grew so large she could barely breathe. Her mouth dried and she began to shake as a surge of adrenalin coursed through her body and made her want to stand up and run.

Finally she understood those movies where the bride bolted...

Then gradually, as if directed by a hand other than her own, she lifted her eyes to the portrait of Stefano's mother, which seemed to glow above the gold fireplace. The beautiful woman there smiled down at her.

My love to you both. The words were as clear as if she were sitting beside the mother-in-law she would never meet. *See only one person or the occasion will overwhelm you.*

Finally Kiki felt the knot that had tied her tongue ease and drift away as if it had never been. *Look, speak and smile at one person and you will be in control of the room.* Kiki sighed and closed her eyes.

When she opened them, the room had narrowed to

the one person who mattered the most—the man she loved with all her heart and who would stand beside her anywhere. Joined to Stefano, she would never be afraid again.

All nervousness fled.

Finally the moment came, and she was so very ready. 'I pledge my life to you, Stefano Adolphi Phillipe Augustus Mykonides.' She smiled. 'My Stefano.'

The Mayor said, 'For ever?'

'I do.'

And they were wed.

When they stepped out onto the balcony of the palace the square below it was filled with Stefano's people— her people now—and the roar of the crowd swelled like the roar of a train, building in intensity and promising to carry her into a new life and new experiences.

Stefano turned her to him and she lifted her face for their first kiss as man and wife. As his lips touched hers the roar of the crowd doubled until they broke apart and smiled at their world.

On the morning of their cathedral wedding Stefano and Kiki lay entwined, heavily asleep, smiles on their faces and hands clasped.

Elise didn't want to wake them, so she sent Jerome in.

'Wake up!'

The young boy had a part to play today and he wanted to get started.

Four hours later in the bride's chambers it was time to leave for the cathedral. It was good to have Nick's hand to stop her trembling, but Kiki could see that today it seemed her big brother was the more nervous one.

Nick had told her that yesterday he'd thought she would faint from fright. He had been worried his little sister had chosen far too public a road for herself. But today she was a new woman, and she could see the look of love and awe on his face and it gave her even more confidence.

Her dress had been created by the principal of a famous Parisian couture house, with lace inserts from its high neck to under her bodice, and sewn with a thousand crystals and the fall of a thousand pearls. The train had her six attendants scurrying, and made Nick shake his head in male confusion.

And the veil… A thousand hours of stitching and twenty yards long, it was so thin and insubstantial it was like looking through a cobweb.

Nick scratched his chin. 'I have no idea how they're going to get this dress into the car.'

Kiki shrugged and twitched her sleeve straight. 'Don't worry. They'll have an expert do it. And it's a very long car.' Already she had learnt.

Her brother raised his brows, threw back his head and laughed.

'What?'

She did not want to be fashionably late. She couldn't wait to see Stefano.

Nick glanced at the open door held by a liveried footman and then back at his radiant sister. 'You've changed.'

She lifted her head. 'I've accepted and I'm blessed.'

She would take everything in her stride. One thing at a time. Because at the end of the day would be Stefano.

'I'm Stefano's wife. I'm going to be a very good one. And I'm not going to worry about the small stuff unless I have to.'

They did get the dress into the Rolls Royce. Just. With a hundred perfect folds so that it would leave the car as beautiful as it had gone in.

The streets were lined with flag-waving residents as Kiki and Nick drove slowly towards the cathedral. They passed huge screens set up on walls to televise the wedding to those outside. In the two cars behind, her six attendants followed: her own three sisters, Nick's wife Tara, two small royal flower girls and one little page boy, smiling so hard the scars on his face shone white in the sunlight.

Jerome's was the face of joy projected around the world which encompassed the celebration for the people in the streets. Finally their favourite prince had wed. They loved their new princess, and they were all invited.

Stefano arrived at the cathedral first, and the crowd roared their approval that he had shunned protocol and chosen to arrive first and wait for his commoner wife. He turned, waved, and entered the building.

Theros accompanied him nervously down the long red carpet to the marble altar at the front. Every red velvet seat was taken. Every foot of space was jammed with bodies and cameras.

Theros kept patting his pocket, where the rings sat. He and Marla had eloped to avoid this very spectacle. This was frighteningly huge.

Nervous of crowds, and frightened of the cathedral,

he was diffident about following his brother, but his own bride had been so sure he could do it and he was determined he would.

Stefano recognised his brother's distress. 'Thank you for standing by me, Theros.' He looked around and spoke quietly, so the microphones wouldn't pick it up. 'I wanted to marry here. Mama is here, and I want her to meet my new princess.'

Then the music started, played by the minstrels in the gallery on golden horns: a serenade on the bride's arrival. Stefano felt his heart trip. So much he had asked of a woman not born to this, and to every new challenge she had risen, teaching him so much about true inner strength. So brave was his bride, and he could not wait for her to stand here beside him and before God.

Then she was at the door, on the arm of his new brother-in-law.

She was a vision. An angel in white with her head high. Through the fine mist of her veil her eyes were searching, finding his, and the music swelled. But it was no match for the swelling in his heart as the woman of his dreams walked slowly towards him. Everything else faded. There was just this woman, fearlessly announcing to the world that she would love him for ever.

As he would love her.

* * * * *

ROMANCE

Playing the Dutiful Wife	Carol Marinelli
The Fallen Greek Bride	Jane Porter
A Scandal, a Secret, a Baby	Sharon Kendrick
The Notorious Gabriel Diaz	Cathy Williams
A Reputation For Revenge	Jennie Lucas
Captive in the Spotlight	Annie West
Taming the Last Acosta	Susan Stephens
Island of Secrets	Robyn Donald
The Taming of a Wild Child	Kimberly Lang
First Time For Everything	Aimee Carson
Guardian to the Heiress	Margaret Way
Little Cowgirl on His Doorstep	Donna Alward
Mission: Soldier to Daddy	Soraya Lane
Winning Back His Wife	Melissa McClone
The Guy To Be Seen With	Fiona Harper
Why Resist a Rebel?	Leah Ashton
Sydney Harbour Hospital: Evie's Bombshell	Amy Andrews
The Prince Who Charmed Her	Fiona McArthur

MEDICAL

NYC Angels: Redeeming The Playboy	Carol Marinelli
NYC Angels: Heiress's Baby Scandal	Janice Lynn
St Piran's: The Wedding!	Alison Roberts
His Hidden American Beauty	Connie Cox

0213 GEN STD HB

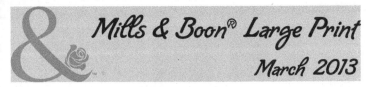

Mills & Boon® Large Print

March 2013

ROMANCE

A Night of No Return	Sarah Morgan
A Tempestuous Temptation	Cathy Williams
Back in the Headlines	Sharon Kendrick
A Taste of the Untamed	Susan Stephens
The Count's Christmas Baby	Rebecca Winters
His Larkville Cinderella	Melissa McClone
The Nanny Who Saved Christmas	Michelle Douglas
Snowed in at the Ranch	Cara Colter
Exquisite Revenge	Abby Green
Beneath the Veil of Paradise	Kate Hewitt
Surrendering All But Her Heart	Melanie Milburne

HISTORICAL

How to Sin Successfully	Bronwyn Scott
Hattie Wilkinson Meets Her Match	Michelle Styles
The Captain's Kidnapped Beauty	Mary Nichols
The Admiral's Penniless Bride	Carla Kelly
Return of the Border Warrior	Blythe Gifford

MEDICAL

Her Motherhood Wish	Anne Fraser
A Bond Between Strangers	Scarlet Wilson
Once a Playboy…	Kate Hardy
Challenging the Nurse's Rules	Janice Lynn
The Sheikh and the Surrogate Mum	Meredith Webber
Tamed by her Brooding Boss	Joanna Neil

Mills & Boon® Hardback
April 2013

ROMANCE

Master of her Virtue	Miranda Lee
The Cost of her Innocence	Jacqueline Baird
A Taste of the Forbidden	Carole Mortimer
Count Valieri's Prisoner	Sara Craven
The Merciless Travis Wilde	Sandra Marton
A Game with One Winner	Lynn Raye Harris
Heir to a Desert Legacy	Maisey Yates
The Sinful Art of Revenge	Maya Blake
Marriage in Name Only?	Anne Oliver
Waking Up Married	Mira Lyn Kelly
Sparks Fly with the Billionaire	Marion Lennox
A Daddy for Her Sons	Raye Morgan
Along Came Twins...	Rebecca Winters
An Accidental Family	Ami Weaver
A Date with a Bollywood Star	Riya Lakhani
The Proposal Plan	Charlotte Phillips
Their Most Forbidden Fling	Melanie Milburne
The Last Doctor She Should Ever Date	Louisa George

MEDICAL

NYC Angels: Unmasking Dr Serious	Laura Iding
NYC Angels: The Wallflower's Secret	Susan Carlisle
Cinderella of Harley Street	Anne Fraser
You, Me and a Family	Sue MacKay

0313 GEN STD HB

Mills & Boon® Large Print

April 2013

ROMANCE

HISTORICAL

MEDICAL